ON CHASING
BRAD THROUGH
PURGATORY

ON CHASING
BRAD THROUGH
PURGATORY

A Novel

STEPHEN BENATAR

Cover design by Kat JK Lee

ISBN: 978-1-5040-2139-5

Distributed in 2015 by Open Road Distribution
345 Hudson Street
New York, NY 10014
www.openroadmedia.com

On Chasing Brad Through Purgatory

1

IT WAS SHORTLY AFTER TWO WHEN WE LEFT THE PARTY. The year—
2005. It was a good party and showed no signs of flagging but Brad
had to be up again by eight. Well such is life: I couldn't remember
when either of us had last had to make an early start on a Sunday.
But his daughter's plane was due in at ten and he was picking her
up at Heathrow.

"Still. Always best to leave while you're having a good time," he
said. He took his hand off the steering wheel and laid it briefly over
mine.

I yawned. "Oh really? I never heard that one before."

He looked at me quietly for a couple of seconds and I saw the hint
of worry encroaching on relaxed good humour. "You *were* having a
good time?" he checked.

"Yes very. Sorry if I sounded tetchy." The car swerved slightly. "Are
you really okay to drive?"

He smiled and nodded. "I truly didn't drink so much. That thar
was nothing but a blip."

The headlights made the narrow country road seem eerie. Trees
lined our route on either side, their branches forming a canopy. I

thought of smugglers in a secret passage. I had recently read *Moon-fleet.*

Normally we would never have driven to a party but the one-man taxi firm in the village had been booked up. I'd already been on my way to the shower when I'd asked at what time John was coming to collect us. Brad had stared and exclaimed and then gone straight to the telephone. The second and third small company he'd tried had also been booked up. "Oh fuck it Danny. I get the feeling someone's trying to tell us something."

"Yes. That each of us shouldn't always rely on the other to look after details."

"But I *like* relying on you. And I like having you rely on me."

He'd held out his arms and I'd walked into them with a well-is-there-any-hope-for-either-of-us type laugh. I'd underlined this: "Despite the obvious pitfalls in such a situation?"

"Yep. Don't be defeatist. The only thing you have to do is brush up on your telepathic skills."

"Hmm. Or you brush up on yours!"

"I shall of course. Christ! One of us has such a startlingly beautiful nature."

"And one of us can be such a total pain in the ass."

Now he said, "Just look at that incredible moon. Both in the sky and on the water." We were out from underneath the canopy and were passing a great gleaming stretch of lake in which the moon floated in devastating clarity. Brad pulled onto a verge and without saying anything we both unfastened our seat belts and walked across the road. We stood with my arm resting on his shoulders and his encircling my waist.

Eventually he spoke. "If this could only be photographed in any way that would ever do it justice!"

"Perhaps that's why God invented painters," I said. "And the writers of fairy tales." I simply meant there was something magical about the scene: geese could turn into princes, witches could be put to rout.

He laughed. "Perhaps that's why the writers of fairy tales invented God."

"Oh yes? What is?"

Yet after a moment he shrugged. "I may have been *moderately* abstemious this evening but you can't expect me actually to think, can you, as well as try to appear clever?"

"Huh!" I said. But, apart from that, I wasn't in the mood to let him bait me. "And we ourselves could maybe form a part of this painting? *The Watchers on the Bank*," I suggested.

"Oh, don't let's give it a title," he said.

"Why not?"

"Cheesy." He gave my waist a squeeze—I saw it as censorious.

"I don't follow you. But in any case," I lied, "it wasn't a title. Only a comment concerning our sadly ineffectual place in the whole vast scheme of things. My place anyway." A person talks such nonsense at half-past-two in the morning, with several fine wines inside him and a substantial amount of one equally fine spirit.

"Ah! You're saying then that we actually *have* a place in the whole vast scheme of things?" Brad's surprise was exaggerated. "Well I ask you now: what could ever illustrate better the yawning gulf between callow youth and worldly-wise maturity and judgment?" The weariness of his sigh was also exaggerated.

So as I say—nonsense, emanating from both sides. I was twenty-six; he was forty-five.

"Worldly-wise judgment," I scoffed. "Just now you had the nerve to accuse me of being cheesy—"

"No! Never!"

"—and please don't interrupt. I need to make a point."

"Yes?"

But for the instant I'd forgotten what my point was. Blast! He twisted round and held me in a warm impulsive hug.

Yet I refused to be silenced.

"Ah yes *cheesy!*" We neither of us pulled away. My cheek rested against his and I now grew pleasantly aware of the cologne we both used although I could never smell it on myself. "In this situation," I said, "wouldn't it take a truly remarkable photographer not to introduce at least an *element* of kitsch? What ought to come out as stunning in its naturalness and beauty just runs the risk of turning cheaply sentimental as soon as you throw in two attractive guys in dinner jackets.

And I don't think even a painter could altogether avoid this." I'd lost sight of the fact I was demolishing my own argument.

And so had he. "Oh, I don't know. When you remember that picture we saw of Narcissus staring at his own reflection in a pool . . ."

Now I did pull away and didn't wait for him to terminate his pause. "Are you calling me Narcissus?"

"No."

I wasn't sure that I believed him. "Then you're deliberately confusing the issue."

"What is the issue? I feel you'll need to remind me. I am sorry."

"No you're not; you don't look in the least bit sorry."

"Are we quarrelling?"

"Yes."

Not very seriously so—as my fist against his cheek suggested—but all the same a wrong note had been struck; and after a minute Brad remembered how late it was.

"There!" I said. "You see? It did remind you of some tacky old Porsche commercial."

"Shut up. Be good. Take one last look and let the magic fill your soul."

But already the moon in the lake had lost something of its power. I couldn't admit to this though. It would have been the same as admitting how pathetically shallow I was. Instead I stood at the car door and drew Brad's attention to the stars. "Why should the moon get all the glory?"

"I love you," said Brad.

"Yes that seems a fitting sort of answer. I love you too by the way."

We buckled up and Brad switched on the engine. "I agree with you. It's sad: how we come to take the stars for granted." That was the phrase which had been going through my own mind; he might already have been honing all those telepathic skills. I regarded his well-chiselled profile with its fine classic nose and smoothly shaven skin, his thick head of naturally shiny hair, basically black but touched all over with becoming grey, the deepening crow's-foot at the hazel eye, and I experienced such a powerful surge of affection that it actually brought forth a patina of tears and I was glad his gaze was on the road. With my forefinger I stroked his shapely dark-haired wrist and vaguely hoped my fingertip might exude a love-lyric worthy of Tennyson or Keats.

I was a humble lad. I knew I couldn't aim as high as Shakespeare.

"In fact when I first came here from London," he said, "I practically made a vow I would stare at the stars in wonder every night. And I was going to buy a staggeringly expensive telescope."

We looked at one another and smiled. Then suddenly: "Hey! *Tears?*" he exclaimed. "Are you all right?"

"I'm fine. Just tears of happiness."

Before he turned away, my own wrist—shapely I hoped and fairly tanned but more or less hairless—received an answeringly fond touch from him.

"I bet that's one of the things that'll impress Suzanne," he said. "I don't suppose she often gets away from Paris. The stars in deepest darkest Sussex ought to come as quite a revelation to her."

Deepest darkest Sussex was represented just then by tall hedgerows on either side of the road. "And what are the other things you think might be going to impress her?" I was hoping I myself would head the list.

"Are you nervous?" he asked.

"You're damned right I am."

"I suppose it'd be a bit strange if you weren't."

"Then why ask?"

"Support. Solidarity. Empathy. I'm feeling nervous too."

I smiled. "I suppose it'd be a bit strange if you weren't."

Perhaps surprisingly this was the one aspect of Suzanne's visit we hadn't discussed. Brad and Hélène had split up four years ago when Suzanne was eighteen. A few months afterwards Hélène had taken her to live in Paris. Despite the separation (because of it said Brad) Brad and his wife remained on good terms and Suzanne had twice come to stay with him in London.

But for their third reunion Brad had gone to Paris and that was the time he'd felt he must let them know the truth; had consequently mentioned me. He and Hélène had been sipping Pernods at a pavement café. "So what's new?" she'd inquired, following his initial revelation, and when Suzanne had joined them from a shopping expedition:

"Darling we were right; but your father's only just made it official." Then his wife and daughter had raised a glass to him and had even included myself in their toast. Hélène had been deeply involved by then with a German businessman, but even so, Brad claimed, this must have rated as one of the easiest comings-out on record, both then and afterwards, despite the keenness of his apprehension.

Yet the thing was, Suzanne hadn't seen him here since his removal into Sussex and my own removal into both his home and—we hoped—the rest of his life. What might have seemed wonderfully simple to accept in the abstract could become a good deal more distressful when faced with certain practicalities. For instance would she and I get on? And when she actually saw, or was in close proximity to, someone taking the place in her father's bed which had once belonged to her mother, mightn't the reality hit home in a way that no amount of distant sophistication and good will could ever quite prepare you for? And she was only four years younger than me. Could that in itself be something of a problem?

Besides I had my pride: I hoped she'd like me and wouldn't be carrying back any sneaky little tales across the Channel. However nice her mum might be. My predecessor.

"She will like you," Brad said. "I shouldn't be surprised if before long she doesn't love you."

"Uh-huh. So that explains why you too are feeling nervous? Yes I can understand that."

"Look. Even though one knows something will work it still doesn't stop one being a bit on edge. Think of all those dinner parties we've given. And really Danny she's such a sweet girl, you've no idea, three minutes after she's here you'll wonder why you worried."

"Why *we* worried."

"God you're stubborn! You don't ever let go do you? But anyway what's the worst that can happen? You end up loathing each other. The whole week is an unmitigated nightmare . . ."

"You and I quarrel. Violently."

"No," he said, "neither probable nor possible. And as for the rest of it . . . nobody's life would be ruined. Not even mine. Though undoubtedly there'd be a sadness." He paused. "But in any case—I repeat—it isn't going to be like that. She's a really sweet girl."

"And I'm a really sweet guy. Seems we were made for one another. We'll probably fall in love and leave you with nothing but the subject for another play."

"I don't know if you've noticed. I write comedies."

He said it with a smile but somehow I again had the feeling there could be some underlying dig. And more than anything else this showed me Brad was under stress despite his allegedly hundred-years-hence sort of attitude: a hundred years hence what will any of this matter? (Before we'd met one of his plays had even been given that as a title.) I thought I made a pretty smooth transition.

"Oh talking of plays you don't suppose there'd be any chance of that new American musical do you?"

"The one which opened at Drury Lane all of three days ago? Well Danny what do you think?"

"Returns?"

"Some hope! And if you even dare to mention ticket touts I'll make you leave this car."

"As bad as that?"

"Slimy profiteering scumbags."

I said drily: "I suppose we couldn't find one who was marginally less slimy? Because if it's a question of paying slightly over the odds for an experience which Suzanne may never have again—certainly not while it's new and fresh and being talked about—then I for one feel that it could conceivably be money well spent."

"You do, do you? Perhaps it doesn't surprise me. Just so long as . . ."

But he didn't finish. Didn't need to. We'd been through all of this a dozen times before. After the last occasion I had foolishly believed that we'd got rid of it forever. I had relaxed my guard.

Just so long as it's other people's money.

We'd had a good time. We'd had a truly good time. How was it possible then that on a fairly brief journey home—half an hour at the outside even allowing for our stop by the lake—how was it possible that such a note of sourness could so suddenly have erupted out of nowhere? Threatening to become the most abiding memory of the entire evening?

But Brad was hurrying on.

"Still we could always fall back on *The History Boys*—we both said we'd be happy to see that again?—or *Guys and Dolls* or perhaps even *Mary Poppins*. We'll get her to choose. And then there'll be things like the Rubens exhibition and that show at the Tate Modern. And restaurants. And tea at the Dorchester. And I suppose we'll have to drive up to my parents' and spend a day there. But we're going to have a wonderful week, the kind of week where we can just play everything by ear and be totally spontaneous and dream up all sorts of happy things we've never done before . . ."

At last, though, he ran out of steam; and turned towards me with a hopeful smile.

"You bastard," I whispered. There were now tears running freely down my cheeks but just then they were not tears of happiness.

"Oh Danny!" he said. "Oh darling! Don't! It was only meant to be humorous—just came out sounding so wrong. I wouldn't do anything in this world to hurt you—oh sweetheart you must realize that? You know you're life itself to me, dearer than life itself?" His tone was almost unbearably full of anguish; unbearably I mean even for me. "I love you," he said.

I was going to tell him I loved him too. It wasn't worth getting into a pet about; he hadn't meant it. But I didn't tell him. There wasn't time. His were the last words we spoke to one another in the car.

We had veered off the road and smashed into a tree.

2

THE WHOLE OF MY RIGHT-HAND SIDE WAS A MESS: broken arm, shoulder, ribs and leg. I learned later that even at the roadside I'd received treatment. My breathing had been checked, a head wound staunched, evening suit cut away and air pumped into bags already placed around my arm and leg. It was in hospital of course that the splints had been fitted.

When I finally came to I was aware of bright lights, a mouth that was dry and disgusting and a headache that felt like a hangover; quite possibly was. A wall clock opposite my bed told me it was eight-twenty-five but I had no idea whether this meant morning or night. I heard a woman's voice say softly—but urgently—"Doctor he's coming round!"

Then there was a gangling young man with sandy hair. Dressed in a white overall and with a stethoscope hanging from his pocket. "Hello there," he said. "Welcome back." He was holding my left wrist. "How d'you feel? Are you in pain?"

"Brad," I cried.

"Sorry?"

"Where's Brad?"

"You mean—the driver of the car?"

"Yes!"

"Oh he's doing fine," replied the doctor. He let go my wrist. "Now how about giving us your own name?" The nurse picked up a pencil and a board.

My own name seemed so utterly beside the point. But I supplied it—impatiently.

"Well, then, Danny. Do you remember anything about this accident?"

I said: "You're lying to me aren't you?"

"Lying about what? No never mind old chap; just try to take it easy. You've been through a terrifying experience and the essential thing right now—"

"The essential thing right now . . ." I was virtually shouting. "Is he okay? Is Brad okay?"

"Yes I told you Danny—he's fine." But his tone was as unconvincing as it was supposed to be reassuring.

The bastard.

Oh Christ. *Bastard*. That was the very last word I'd spoken to him. Brad. The very last thing I'd ever called him. Oh God he couldn't be. Couldn't be. Oh please God—anything, anything—I'll promise you anything. But don't let Brad be dead.

"Danny there's only one thing you must worry about from now on. Nothing else matters. You've got to concentrate on getting well. You've been badly hurt but you're young and you're strong and there's absolutely no reason why . . ."

Oh God I don't care about getting well. If you want one of us please take me not Brad. I truly don't care about dying.

(Except that if Brad lived 'truly' wasn't entirely true. Still . . . nothing but a quibble, that.)

Yet first I need to talk to him again. Quite briefly. Just to tell him what I didn't have the chance to, what I was on the very point of telling him—

But it was only the doctor who responded.

"We need the telephone number of your next of kin Danny. And then we're going to give you something that will help dull the pain and relax you—get you back to sleep for a while."

You see I need to tell him that I love him. And how very much I love him. And that finding him was the best thing that ever happened to me.

Please.

Besides, God. What about Suzanne? Who'll be there to meet Suzanne?

"This *is* Sunday morning?" I said.

The doctor nodded. "Telephone number?" he asked. He paused—hypodermic pointed ceilingwards. The nurse, who had just swabbed a patch on my left arm, now retrieved her pencil.

"But first you've got to tell me. I need to know what's happened to Brad. Is Brad dead?"

I saw his look of uncertainty.

Yet even then I had to hear it put into words.

"Please," I said. "Just tell me the truth—I'll give you the telephone number, you'll give me the injection and then I'll be your easiest living patient bar none."

Still he hesitated. We watched the excess fluid spurt out of the syringe.

"Danny I repeat it's you who are important now. And for Brad's sake as much as for your own you've got to put all your energies into simply growing strong. But yes old man. I am sorry. Your friend is dead."

3

THE DOCTOR AND THE NURSE BOTH LEFT THE ROOM—maybe only to confer in the corridor but in that case I hoped their conference wouldn't be too brief; I hoped the drug now pumping through my bloodstream would also allow me the several seconds that I needed. But this was slightly more in my control: mind over matter I told myself. *Mind over matter!*

I'd noticed the jug of water and the glass. They were sitting on a bedside locker to my left.

It wasn't difficult to seize that tumbler. It wasn't difficult to bring it crashing down against the locker edge.

Much of the glass remained embedded in my palm—I was hardly aware of it; far more concerned about the noise of breakage. But the vital point was this: between my thumb and forefinger I now retained a good-sized shard.

For I knew where the jugular was; Brad had once shown me when discussing the details of a thriller he'd been reading.

And it seemed wholly right that it was from Brad I should have learned this. Because I couldn't live without Brad. It was as simple as that. I just couldn't live without him.

So. I had assumed he'd died on impact. This would have given him a six-hour start. Roughly. But I thought it likely that if I set out fast enough I'd very soon catch up—my notion of the afterlife included an early reunion of people who had loved each other. Self-evident then: a need for the swiftest possible pursuit. Apart from all else I had to draw the sting out of that very last word he'd heard from me.

'Apart from all else . . .'? What I cared about more than anything just then was the question of our being able to travel through purgatory together. I couldn't bear the thought of his feeling either lonely or homesick or afraid.

Through purgatory.

Towards judgment.

4

INSTINCTIVELY, I knew I was still visible. Therefore I had to hide behind the door when finally the nurse returned. In the end I'd been left alone for something like five minutes; she clearly hadn't heard the shattering of the glass. But she gasped and very nearly screamed when she saw the nasty mess upon the bed: the mortal remains of the late Danny Casement wreathed about in blood and bandaging yet also (to my own eye anyway) wreathed about in tranquillity.

And behind the door I was free of blood and bandaging and splints and saline drip. Free of hangover or headache. I felt light-limbed and even light-hearted. Liberated.

Naturally I was sorry for the shock she'd sustained; and for the vast amount of trouble I might now be causing; but I wasn't sorry when she ran out shakily to summon help. Then I made off swiftly in the opposite direction—at this end the corridor was clear. Through side-doors I saw patients propped up in their beds talking or reading or simply staring into space. Heard a snatch of music from one of the wards: Gladys Knight, "I'd rather live in his world than live without him in mine." This seemed either a remarkably happy coincidence or else a positive message of encouragement—and, reassuringly, that midnight train to Georgia kept running through my head for at least the next hour. It beat time to my lookout for orderlies, beat time to my lookout for clocks. Just thirteen minutes to nine. Great. It hadn't taken long.

I avoided the lift and the obviously busy entrance hall. I was wearing nothing but a gown. I had no wish to be challenged.

Instead I took the stairs and charged down them two-at-a-time until I reached the basement. I was in the right area of the basement; almost at once I found a bolted door that gave onto the outside world: up from the nether regions into the late-October sunlight, a glorious Indian summer which we'd been enjoying for the past three days and had been hoping, Brad and I, would stay constant for Suzanne's visit. So when I grabbed a raincoat hanging on a peg beside the door I was thinking less about exterior temperature than about youthful modesty: those gowns revealed a lot of butt. And I knew the location of the hospital where they'd have brought me—if I wanted to take the shortest route back to the scene of the accident I'd have to pass in full view of the house which served as police station. I had no idea why I needed to return to the scene of the accident. I only knew I did.

I kept to the grass as far as I could; for much of the time on a bank above the road. It wasn't a busy road; it was the same that Brad and I had joined last night, a little further on, out of a rutted and cross-country lane. During the next half-hour no more than a dozen cars went by. I saw two cyclists and an old man with his dog and a schoolboy wearing cap and tie and blazer—despite its being a Sunday. I strode out purposefully but at no point did I run: running would only get me into a sweat and I wanted to retain my cool. My cool, my street cred . . . I almost laughed. I could scarcely have imagined I'd ever be seen dead walking along the queen's highway in nothing but a hospital gown and some grubby bit of gabardine, too tight and barely reaching to my knees. I remembered the perennial childhood cry of myself and my siblings when forced out on a weekend family tramp: "Hope I don't meet anyone I know!" Fifteen years later I again proclaimed it, more cheerfully this time, but now followed it with its antithesis: "Hope I *shall* meet somebody I know!" In fact I actually shouted this more positive version as if I half-believed its sound or sense might carry on the wind to wherever Brad had got by now—maybe not so desperately far ahead—to let him know that I was bearing up. I felt pretty certain he'd be bearing up (gone was my earlier worry that he might be feeling scared). But then it occurred to me not only wasn't there a wind, he wouldn't even be aware of my being so hotly in pursuit. Wouldn't be aware yet that neither of us need journey on alone. I hadn't realized: I had it a good deal easier than him. I tried to push myself still faster.

But despite my speeding and preoccupation I could hardly be impervious to the blue sky and warm sunshine which filtered through the trees. "You know," I had said to him once, "I really can't imagine the sun continuing to shine after I'm dead. I really can't imagine things just carrying on as usual. People doing their shopping; looking to see what's on TV. You're going to say of course that's being immensely arrogant."

"No perish the thought," he'd told me. "I shouldn't dream of saying any such thing."

"Which is just as well you fibber. Because if you think *that's* arrogant I'm afraid you haven't heard the half of it!"

"Then go ahead: shock me. No I'm sorry. I mean educate me."

"I don't know if I dare."

But naturally I did. It was pillow talk; one of those countless occasions when we'd rambled on under cover of darkness about all sorts of unimportant things—and yet who ever knows what might turn out to be important? "I can also find it hard to imagine that the sun ever managed to shine *before* I was born. Honestly! I quite often look up at the sky and think, 'Since the start of human life people have felt the sun on their skins and seen cloud formations just like this and gazed up in wonder at the sunset,' and to say that each time it fills me with surprise might be slightly overstating it but it does give me a little jolt, or frisson. I shouldn't even say since the start of human life. I only have to go back a couple of hundred years to find it all equally astonishing, the fact that people shared the same experiences as me—that other men for example all through the ages have enjoyed orgasms roughly the same as mine. Is that now getting arrogant enough?"

"No you're still an absolute beginner. Just paltry unambitious stuff."

"I think I can do better then."

"Indeed I should hope so."

"I used to believe that I was special—"

"You're intensely special."

"No Brad I mean like Jesus. When I was a boy part of me really thought I was designed to be another saviour; not to die on the cross, nothing uncomfortable like that; but put here on earth to be a fine example to all you sad and ordinary folk. How'm I doing?"

"None too well. That's just sweet and childlike and completely normal. You no doubt believed at least half the time that you were utterly despicable and quite beyond the pale. Much less deserving than any of us poor sad and ordinary folk."

"I did! I did! How can you know these things? How can you be so very wise?"

"I guess because I was designed to be extremely special—oh far more special than yourself. You fake and fraud and upstart!"

"I reckon I must love you then . . . you very wise extremely special man."

"I reckon I must love you too . . . you false and jumped-up boy."

I smiled—then was suddenly surprised to find that in the throes of reminiscence I'd passed unnoticing the place at which seven hours earlier we'd turned into the main road. Brad had been concentrating on all those potentially dangerous ruts; we had hardly spoken until we'd driven to about this point, when I'd lazily mentioned the irony of needing to be up so early on this particular Sunday. "Still. Always best to leave while you're having a good time," he'd said.

And very soon I got to that vaulted section which had reminded me of smugglers but where there was no longer any grassy bank and I was forced for the sake of my soles to tread more carefully. When I reached the other end and came to the spot where we had pulled over and then gone to stand beside the lake, arm around shoulder, arm around waist, I experienced even now a sudden sharp twist of nostalgia—and thought, "My God how good we had it and how much of it I simply took for granted."

Experienced it even now despite my knowing our reunion couldn't be that far off. It struck me forcibly how very blest I was. Under any other circumstances, with Brad gone, I'd have had to avoid this lake altogether, perhaps this whole stretch of road, certainly for the time being. To revisit . . . would have been much more than I could manage. Could I even have borne to go back into the house, although obviously I should have had to? But how did others cope in such a situation? To my shame I knew I'd never given it much thought. Maybe the closest I'd ever come was crying in front of some old movie dealing with bereavement. In my own life only one grandmother had died; and she had been someone to mimic rather than to mourn.

Back in the car. By now we had been talking of Suzanne.

Suzanne . . . ! No doubt at this moment she was somewhere high above the Channel looking forward with a mixture of pleasurable anticipation and suppressed nervousness to a week of holiday spent with her father and his boyfriend. How would she react when no one came to meet her? When no one answered her increasingly panicked calls? Suppose for some reason she couldn't get in touch with her mum back in Paris—and in any case what could Hélène reasonably advise? Suzanne was only twenty-two; she was going to feel so let down and lost and helpless. And all because some schmuck had called her father a bastard. Dear God look after her.

Part of me, undoubtedly a part which needed to grow up, provided for her a young airport official, handsome and unattached and caring, who would tactfully take control. Man made in God's own image. During slack periods at work—I'd worked on the reception desk of a small hotel in Uckfield—I sometimes used to read romantic novels; even, despite the teasing, Mills & Boon. I'd claim these made a change from heavier things like Gide and Kafka and Joyce and Pasternak though no one at the hotel ever saw me with Gide or Kafka or Joyce or Pasternak. (But you did Brad. You did. Sorry if in the end I had to return each time to the more lightweight stuff and never let you know.) But please God. Just for Suzanne. This once. You ever read a Mills & Boon?

(Daft question. The million times you must have helped to write one.)

The association of ideas inevitably brought into my mind Sebastian and Sally and Laura. Gosh would the three of them be shaken! Imagining this, made me almost laugh again. Oh to be a fly on the wall—my grandmother's reiterated wish—when somehow the news got through to The White Hart! I reflected that throughout their lives they'd fleetingly remember me, those three; remember me as bright-eyed, blond and sexy and always in tiptop physical condition. Not bad, that; there were certain consolations in nearly everything; although I knew I shouldn't care.

I supposed I'd soon be seeing my grandmother. The prospect didn't thrill me. "Don't do this . . . don't do that . . . I'd have hoped you would have learned by now!" My chief remembrance of her. Negatives.

Yet now the thought came rushing: I had no right to mimic her as cruelly as I did. Admittedly, only in front of my brothers and sisters but not merely before she'd died—even afterwards as well. Soon afterwards. And with the same total lack of understanding. I wished I'd never done it. I really wished I'd never done it.

Something else, not simply a thought, that came rushing on me just as unexpectedly: that bend in the road where the bark of a massive lone oak was jaggedly damaged near its base—the naked wood savagely indented; where there were tyre marks on the verge, and bits of broken glass among the fallen leaves.

Yet that was all. They had removed the Porsche with commendable efficiency; I briefly wondered where. Less briefly I wondered where they had taken the body of its driver. Most likely to the same place where they had taken mine; or now were taking it. But what would happen to us after that?

Of course if I had an actual preference we would both be buried side-by-side in the nearby peaceful pretty churchyard—St Leonard's which I had from time to time attended—with a gravestone common to the pair of us; but even if there'd been room in the churchyard and the coupling of male lovers on a single stone could now at last be countenanced there still remained the problem that Brad had been a non-believer. I would willingly have gone with him to the nearest cemetery, naturally, though the nearest cemetery couldn't start to compare aesthetically with the churchyard at St Leonard's but I had never made a will—what had I to leave?—I didn't know if Brad had either, and never having discussed with any of our friends or family the issue of interment as opposed to cremation (had Brad ever done so in the days before I knew him?), I now wasn't at all sure where any of this muddle finally left us or whether indeed—

Oh Christ!

Brad wasn't a believer.

How could I have forgotten? How could I have overlooked that glaringly important point?

He had been such a good man.

God! God! God! He was such a good man. A dozen times better than me. More! Oh Lord you can't refuse him his salvation just because he honestly couldn't understand why if you existed you permitted such a quantity of suffering. It would be so petty to deny him. To deny membership to someone merely because he didn't tug his forelock when in every other way, apart from the actual card-carrying bit, he practised all your teachings just as truly as any person ever could! You *can't* deprive him of the same chances which you're supplying to a nobody like me! Oh Lord, Lord. You who so clearly understand everything. And isn't understanding the same thing as forgiving? You can't possibly be a lesser soul—a meaner, touchier, stubborner soul—than whoever it was who said that. Wasn't it a Frenchman?

Arrogance? I'm afraid you haven't heard the half of it.

And listen God—Lord—I've never known which one I should be talking to. If you insist on sticking to these rules . . . belief, belief, belief! . . . then count me out. As of *this* minute. I don't want to be in any place where Brad himself can't be. I don't want any part of a life which he himself can't share. I don't want any further dealings with a God who's so very obviously a clubman.

No thank you. I'll just go along with Gladys. I'd rather die in his world than live without him in mine.

I licked my lips realizing I had made a declaration of such life-threatening seriousness I ought at least to formalize it.

If Brad isn't somewhere on the road ahead I hereby give notice that as of this moment I'm officially withdrawing my allegiance. It's as if I no longer believe.

There now. Come on and strike me dead.

In spite of everything I rather enjoyed the wording of that last command. The situation hardly permitted of a grin; I was well aware of that; but it got one just the same. My whole approach must seem so vain, my puerile little ultimatum so irredeemably . . . puerile. Yet so far I was still standing. So far I was still breathing. No thunderbolt, no interruption to that gently warming sun. What could I do but hope then that I might have had my answer?

Yet like nothing short of an overindulged brat I again decided to test how far I'd be allowed to go.

I said: Then just so long as we understand each other? No crossed fingers; no dirty tricks; no pretending afterwards you hadn't fully grasped my meaning.

Some sort of a sign wouldn't be bad. Some little token of good faith.

Like a bit of skywriting perhaps? *Brad lives!* You don't even need an aeroplane. Only dip your finger in a trailing wisp of cloud or else some garden bonfire smoke. *Brad lives. Just follow the yellow brick road.*

I looked about me. Like I say I was at the scene of the accident. Pure instinct had returned me.

But just for the moment—I hoped just for the moment—pure instinct appeared to be stalling. No skywriting. No yellow brick road. Merely a bend and a tree and granules of glass catching the sunlight between the fallen leaves.

So what now I wonder.

5

AND A HOUSE.

Bend—tree—glass—leaves. And a house.

It was on the other side of the road some twenty yards back and well hidden behind a weathered brick wall that reached above my head. The wrought-iron gates revealed a sweep of gravel drive, tree-lined and culminating round a circular island of lawn behind which was the front door, shiny and bottle-green. As far as I could see it was the only house in that immediate area. Viewed from the gates it looked impressive, even daunting.

Especially to someone who wore a raincoat that was stained and several sizes too small and had nothing showing below other than bare legs and feet.

I walked up the drive. A dog barked. I looked for a sign that might direct me to the tradesmen's entrance.

A middle-aged woman in a dressing gown opened the front door. I hadn't even knocked. She was plump, fair-haired, had a pleasant sort of face and held a snarling mastiff by the collar; held it so tightly that its forepaws no longer touched the ground.

"I'm sorry," she said, "no hawkers or . . ."

I wondered what might have come next. Probably beggars though she was too polite to say it. It obviously couldn't have been Jehovah's Witnesses or encyclopedia salesmen or double-glazing representatives. At least I hoped not—for *their* sakes.

"But if you wait a minute," she said, "I could go and make you a cheese sandwich."

"That's very kind but I'm really not here to ask for handouts."

She was impressed by my voice as I had hoped she would be. And perhaps also by my face now that she had heard my voice. If it hadn't been for that shattered tumbler my face might well have been black-eyed and badly bruised; but to judge from my hands and legs and feet death seemed mercifully to have got rid of all such marks of injury. Had it also got rid of the need for food I now wondered briefly, at her mention of a sandwich. I thought that probably it hadn't: I could in fact have fancied a cheese sandwich or more particularly the cooked breakfast which Brad and I had usually allowed ourselves on a Sunday. Not that in any case, I remembered, we'd have had much time for any cooked breakfast this morning.

Also while I'd been approaching the house and feeling somewhat nervous it had occurred to me I'd like a pee. But then the dog had barked so there was no longer any question of my simply stepping up behind a tree or bush. Anyway the urgency had now departed.

"Then how may I help?"

"I'm sorry to be a nuisance," I said, "but in the small hours of this morning there was a car accident across the road. I'm wondering if by any chance you—"

"Yes we did!" she said. "My God! It was horrific. That bang . . . we almost thought the world had ended!"

"Esther what is it?" A male voice from above.

"Someone inquiring about the accident," she called back though scarcely turning her head. "All right Rufus please stop. You can stop now." She relaxed her hold upon the dog's collar and the animal stood properly on its four legs. It made a sound that was either one of compliance or of disappointment or possibly both.

Her balding rather squat and jowly husband (I assumed) with grey bristles in his ears and sleep in his eyes, having descended the remainder of the stairs, now came to take a look at the person who was making these inquiries. He wore blue silk pyjamas and black leather slippers. I said quickly, "I have to apologize for my appearance but it's a long story."

"What do you need to know about the accident?"

To be candid, I could have said, I haven't the slightest idea. But then somehow I managed to find the right words.

"I knew the man who was driving."

"Oh God!" said the woman.

"The poor devil," said her husband.

"Would you like to come in?" asked the woman. They all moved aside to make room—although Rufus, until his mistress yanked him hurriedly away, stuck an upwardly inquiring nose under the bottom of the raincoat. I wiped my feet on the doormat but still left damp prints across the varnished floor. They led me into their kitchen and towards a scrubbed deal table flanked by wooden benches. Two filled cups and saucers waited on a small tray. It was the husband who fetched another cup and brought the teapot from the stove. It seemed almost farcical to be answering his questions to do with milk and sugar. (But that's exactly what I meant Brad. We're dead yet life goes on. In all its mundanity. Be truthful now—that can't be right! Surely?)

"Did you know him well?" the husband asked.

"Yes. Very. Brad was in every way my closest friend."

And let them make what they liked of that. We had never been ones to flaunt our sexuality but we had never been ones to feel ashamed of it either.

"I'm so dreadfully sorry," said the wife—Esther. "Really so dreadfully sorry."

"Thank you. In fact I shouldn't be letting myself use that past tense. I feel he still *is* my closest friend. And always will be. Don't just feel it either; actually *know* it!"

"That's certainly a good way to look at it," she said—after a short but distinctly awkward silence. Her husband nodded gravely.

I helped myself to sugar and I saw them notice my hands: the fact that they were well looked after. I hoped this did something further to counteract the effect of my very weird apparel.

"He had his son with him didn't he Rob?" The woman turned back to me. "At least that's what we thought but clearly you'd know better than us."

"No, Brad hadn't got a son, just a daughter." I glanced up again at the electric clock. Twenty to ten or thereabouts.

Naturally we couldn't see him all that well. A young man something like yourself. Same sort of colouring. Face a bit smashed up. Oh dear. But they said he had a chance—the paramedics."

It was then that I heard about the treatment I'd received at the roadside; it made me feel both grateful and a bit shifty.

"They were really brilliant, those two, so very calm and capable, I don't know how they do it. It was Rob of course who got them here in the first place—well no I mean it was the police who did that but it was Rob who . . ." She seemed to be getting confused and Rob reached across and mutely took her hand. "Oh it was dreadful," she said. Her eyes began to swim. "You feel so absolutely helpless."

"There was nothing you could do sweetheart. And it didn't take long before we heard the siren. It just *seemed* like for ever. And they always say . . . well that you should never disturb anything. You see"— Rob was now speaking to me—"she so much wanted to do something but I wouldn't let her and I felt really mean about that."

"Yet I'm certain you were right," I murmured; though more to her than to him. "Broken bones et cetera. But it must be very hard."

"And at least we didn't just walk away from it," said Rob. "Not like that precious toff in his fancy evening suit!"

Rufus was sniffing round my ankles. My hand had been halfway towards him; I'd been meaning to stroke him on the top of his head.

"I'm sorry?"

"This man we saw." It was Esther who answered. "He was standing at the next bend in the road. Only twenty yards or so from where the thing had happened. Looking back; hesitant; definitely unsure about something. He stood full in the moonlight so we got a good view of him. Even though he turned and walked away almost immediately."

"But you say . . . you say he was wearing a dinner jacket?"

"And what I also say—," interjected Rob.

Yet for the moment his wife was concentrating more on me and maybe unwittingly cut across him. "Yes. Just like the two in the car were. It's right what they always claim, you know. About truth being stranger than fiction."

"And what I also say," repeated Rob, "is that it must have been him who caused the accident."

"Oh no you don't know that," protested his wife forcefully. "You really don't know that."

"Why else should the car have swerved so suddenly? Because that fellow crossed the road without a second's warning and of course the driver did his best to avoid him. But he wasn't worth trying to save if you ask me. A man who can just walk away from an accident—any accident that's unattended but especially one for which you yourself have been responsible! I told the police, let Constable York know *precisely* how I felt, when we gave them that description . . ."

"But you just don't know," repeated his wife. "He had a nice face. Kind. He looked . . . well just so anxious; so concerned. He really seemed enormously reluctant to have to leave."

"Sweetheart I don't care how enormously reluctant he seemed. The main thing is—he left."

"There could have been a reason."

"Like what?"

I said: "That description you gave them. May I hear it too?" I had been careful not to rush in; I was having a struggle to keep my expression suitably composed. "Maybe I know him?"

"Well as I've already told you—he was a toff in an evening suit. But it's a wonder we noticed even that much. It was the middle of the night, remember. We'd just stumbled through our gate after being shocked awake by the sound of a tremendous smash. It was obviously the accident itself which concerned us."

"He was a man of about forty," said Esther, "or he might have been a bit older. He was tall and very handsome and had a good figure and dark hair . . ." She petered out, perhaps conscious that in the circumstances it was indeed a little strange she should have registered so much, or else wondering if such details at such a time might not strike us as slightly inappropriate. There'd been a renewed element of defiance in her tone, even of near-hysteria; I somehow got the feeling that

Constable York hadn't paid her the same degree of attention which he'd accorded to her husband. "Oh he was probably just here for the weekend," she concluded, almost bathetically.

"Why do you say that?"

Why do you say that oh you wonderful woman?

"Because if he were local we'd have recognized him, dinner jacket or not. Not that we've been here very long ourselves—only a couple of months—so possibly that's why—"

"Well if that's the case thank God for small mercies. Sweetheart you might like him as a neighbour. But me—no way—not in a million years."

Rob smoothed one stubby-fingered and reflective hand over his balding pate. Again turned back to me.

"As a matter of fact," he said, "I gave this handsome fellow chase. But not at once of course and when I did I'd left it far too late. At the very least, you see, he must have been a witness."

"You gave him chase? I'm not sure I'd have thought of that."

"But I hadn't felt happy about leaving Esther; that was the crux of it. Not to mention not being in the pink of condition! And when I did dash round the corner he was almost out of sight. I was just in time to see him turning off towards Pack Hill and if it hadn't been for the moonlight I mightn't even have seen that much. God knows what he was going to do up there at half-past-two in the morning! Heading for some witches' coven as like as not. Definitely up to no good!"

Again I wanted to express my joy; would have liked to dance or cry out in gratitude. I had been asking for a sign. At first it had seemed I wasn't going to get one but now I'd been given not just a sign but even an eyewitness account—*two* eyewitness accounts—with virtually a road map thrown in. Glorious and irrefutable proof I'd soon be catching up with Brad.

"But aside from witches' covens," I said, "there's nothing very much up Pack Hill is there? I've only been there once; even the views were disappointing. The only *vaguely* interesting thing was a pile of ruins which somebody told us was the site of an ancient hostelry—afterwards we looked it up in the local library. Odd sort of place to have an inn! But apparently in its heyday it used to draw people from all over. Pilgrims and whatnot. It was called The Halfway House."

Perhaps my relief was causing me to burble. Esther stifled a yawn. She gave a guilty smile. "They asked us if we wanted sleeping pills. I think we were sensible to accept but all the same . . ."

"Please don't apologize; I should be off anyway. Thank you for the tea. And thank you for . . . well for everything you did or would have liked to do."

The three of us stood up. Rufus reluctantly stopped licking my feet and scrambled to his own. I gave his ears a farewell rub.

But in the hall I hesitated.

"Is there any chance I might briefly use your phone? I'm afraid I couldn't pay for it but I need to call Heathrow to try to get a message to Brad's daughter."

Afterwards, when we'd already shaken hands and I was standing on the doorstep, Esther remembered something. "I meant to ask. Do you also know the young man who was injured?"

"Yes," I said.

"Know him well?"

I didn't answer for a moment. "I always thought I did. Now I'm not so sure."

They may have taken this to mean I felt disappointed in him and that in some way his behaviour had let me down or let Brad down. If so I wasn't too unhappy just to leave it there.

"Will you be visiting him in hospital?"

"As a matter of fact I've just left the hospital."

"And how was he?"

I merely shrugged; not wishing to add any further to their aftermath of sadness.

"But do you think he might like Rob and me to go and visit?"

"I'm afraid he died." I said it as gently as I could.

"Oh no!"

The tears now spilled over in earnest. She held her hands before her face. Rob put his arm around her shoulders.

"I am so *sorry*," she sobbed.

"Don't be. Please don't be. It was absolutely for the best."

"Why?" Rob asked. "Was he brain-damaged?" .

"No it wasn't that." I paused and strived for something that would bring them comfort. "Really. It was what he wanted. Wanted more than anything." I threw in all the conviction which the sheer truth of it merited.

The trouble was an instant later I heard the echo of my own words. And realized that I hadn't said 'he'. I had said 'I'.

Esther had taken her hands down. Little surprise then that I saw in both their faces the dawning of a drastically reconsidered opinion of me.

Perhaps I should have tried to explain. But I didn't feel *I'm sorry that was just a slip of the tongue* would really have been adequate and I couldn't think of anything else. I left them believing I must be wholly without feeling. Vengeful even. I was thoroughly dismayed. I liked them both and they'd been kind to me. And I didn't want them turning cynical on my account, possibly being less inclined to offer hospitality to strangers.

Though maybe in regard to myself it was simply poetic justice. At some points in my life 'wholly without feeling' might nearly have been right. So let me be condemned now for all the times I'd previously managed to get away with it. Didn't that seem fair?

Anyhow I tried to be philosophical; told myself not to exaggerate—or dramatize—my own influence.

6

IT WAS A STEEPER CLIMB THAN I REMEMBERED—though previously of course we'd travelled up by car. I estimated that the winding road must have been well over a mile but I tackled it with vigour and was pleased to find I wasn't out of breath on reaching the top.

The first thing I noticed was the view; how could I have thought Pack Hill not worthy of a second visit? From its crest you could probably see across four counties; you could certainly glimpse the far-off sparkle of the English Channel. Why'd I been under the impression there were countless rows of new development obstructing the horizon?

The second was even more challenging; or would have been had I not been able to adjust to it faster. The Halfway House wasn't in ruins any longer. It had become precisely the sort of old inn with fresh white paint and window boxes and character and charm you might dream of finding at lunchtime on a weekend drive. Overlooking the village green perhaps or else the duck pond in the high street. Become *again* I thought.

A man I rightly took to be the manager, more on account of his air of authority than because of any formality in his attire (Bob Presley at

The White Hart would *never* have stood about in jeans where any of the guests might see), leant comfortably against the inn door. He had his arms crossed—ankles too—and looked as if he were simply there to enjoy the sunshine or to entertain some fairly beguiling reverie. But the moment he saw me he straightened up.

"Hi. You must be Danny. I'm Richard."

We shook hands. His face, his height, his breadth of shoulder—the niceness of his smile of welcome—all of this inspired confidence.

"How are you feeling?" he asked.

"Feeling fine," I replied. "And probably I'll be feeling even better when . . ."

"When you've got a little more used to things? Natural enough. You'd hardly be human if you weren't feeling apprehensive."

"No I wasn't going to say that. I was only going to say it really all depends on the answer you're about to give me."

"What's the question?"

"Did a guy named Brad Overton get here all right? At about three this morning? He was wearing a dinner jacket. You couldn't have missed him."

"I wasn't on duty at that time."

"No but you'd know anyway. Surely? There must be records—a computer. You were standing here expecting me."

"I'm sure he'd have arrived okay. But Danny it's yourself you've got to think about. No one else."

Had he been listening to that doctor? My faith in him began to fade. It was almost certain that when people were evasive they were covering up bad news.

I said: "I know that he started up Pack Hill; there was someone who saw him. So having come this far he wouldn't have been turned back would he? Not even if . . . ?" I paused. "That's all I need to hear."

"Not even if what?"

"He didn't believe in God."

"Danny I can't tell you that."

"Why not?"

He didn't answer. Still gave me that pleasant friendly look which I no longer saw, quite, as being either of those things.

"And do you mean that you *can't* or that you *won't*?"

"I'm sorry. I know you're disappointed but I can only repeat what I've already told you. At this point it's yourself and no one but yourself that should concern you."

"He was my partner God damn it!"

"I do sympathize."

"I don't want your sympathy. I want your reassurance. And I was the one who brought about his death. Therefore if it wasn't for me this whole silly question would never have arisen." Well not for another forty years or so but I was now in no mood to let any element of fairness enter into this.

And anyhow who knew what changes mightn't have occurred during the next forty years or so? Concerning that vexed question of belief? I knew I'd have been working on it. Working on it with insidious persistence.

"I feel certain he's going to be all right," said the other—but was it just a question of appeasing me? He turned and opened the inn door. I stayed precisely where I was.

"No. Listen. Would it be a problem?" I was really doing my level best to remain calm. "This whole issue of his non-belief? Because it's quite obvious, isn't it, that the very second he stepped out of the car or at least the very second he realized he'd be capable of doing so he'd have changed into a believer? And knowing Brad he'd have said, 'Dear God how could I have got it all so wrong? What a complete idiot I must have been. I'm so ashamed. Forgive me.' So he wouldn't have been turned away would he? That's all I need to know."

I was aware I was repeating myself. "You're very persistent," said the manager.

"Please Richard."

But he was as repetitive as I was. "There's no way I can hand out guarantees. There just isn't. Again I must apologize." He smiled. "But if you insist on holding up our work much longer I think *you* may be the one having to apologize!"

"Oh sod your work!" It wasn't just the deadlock which caused me to behave like this, it was that grin of his, the knowing charm and warmth of it, fraudulent maybe but at the same time nearly irresistible.

Nor did he react to my explosion. Neither by word nor look. (And anyway, if he had, it wouldn't have made a difference.) "You needn't think I'm moving an inch inside that door unless I know there's going to be some point!"

"Point?" That did seem to surprise him.

"Unless, that is, I know I'm following in the footsteps of Brad Overton. Because the one thing that's more important to me than anything else on earth right now—on earth or in any other place—is to catch up with Brad and tell him that I love him. I'm sorry if that sounds novelettish. I'm a novelettish sort of guy and have novelettish points of view. If he isn't inside here . . . then too bad. I'll have to go and look for him elsewhere."

"Absolutely putting paid to your own chances? You do realize that if you turn away now there's no second chance."

"Oh God in heaven! How can I make you understand? I couldn't give a toss about my own chances."

Richard subjected me to a long hard look. "You really mean that?" he asked, after some considerable pause.

I wasn't even sure that it had been a question but in any case I treated it as such. "You better just believe it," I said.

"Very well."

There was a further lengthy pause.

"Danny of course your friend is okay. Checked in, as you say, at his expected time. At round about three this morning."

Apparent capitulation. Just like that. I knew it had been too easy— far too easy. There were lines we'd had to learn at school: *meet it is I set it down, that one may smile, and smile, and be a villain* . . . "So you're saying he's here? You're telling me I can be taken to him straightaway?"

But it was stupid: notwithstanding my obvious scepticism I still felt a brief stirring of hope.

"No I'm sorry. I'm not telling you that." (Well surprise surprise!) "Brad's already moved on."

"Of course he has," I said. "Evidently very *long* stays here are the kind encouraged."

Almost without knowing it I had backed away. He regarded me with a concern which in spite of everything I could have found convincing.

I pointed at an aerial attached to one of the gables. "That's just for you I take it?"

"For me and for my colleagues," he agreed pleasantly. "Though not entirely so. Occasionally people will stay with us for several days. There's no fixed rule." He added in the same conciliatory tone and with scarcely any break, "Danny you're an awkward little cuss aren't you? I wonder if you realize that."

Well he had charisma—or sex appeal—or the art of persuading you that he was being sincere. Or something. And Christ knows if I couldn't have faith in Richard then I would really be out on a limb. Where on earth would I turn next? Though my own capitulation was a little less graceful than his. "And is that what goes down in my report?" I asked. "Awkward cuss?" Brad had sometimes called me ornery.

"Oh you'd be surprised at what goes down in your report! But don't tell me that finally you may be almost ready to come in?"

"Yet only for a minute or two; I'm afraid I can't stay."

He laughed.

"A minute or two may prove to be something of an understatement," he said. "But only a small one."

"Why do I get the feeling that if anyone actually spent the night here you'd class him as a resident?"

"In fact I'd say—what?—thirty minutes ought to do it comfortably."

"Do what?"

"See to things before you have to start back."

"*Back?*"

"Back to where you've just come from."

"But I thought you said . . ." Already? The resurgence of distrust? "Said that if I turned away now . . ."

"Being ordered back is scarcely the same as turning away of your own accord. And besides. It's purely on a temporary basis; very temporary. But the thing is—you're wearing an article of stolen clothing."

For the first instant I didn't even understand his reference.

"*This?*"

As my thumb and finger plucked at the worthless gabardine my tone betrayed equal amounts of distaste and incredulity.

"Surely it isn't going to ruin anybody's life: the lack of *this*? Or even mildly inconvenience it?"

"You don't know that. And the fact remains—it's stolen property."

"Then the gown I'm wearing underneath must also count as stolen property. Only think how that'll delay my return—I mean my return *here*—when I get arrested and charged with streaking!" In all honesty I found the prospect slightly titillating.

"The gown is standard hospital issue," observed Richard. "No problem about that."

"I'm not too sure I follow your distinction."

"And in any case you're now going to be given some new clothes. Let's find Hermione."

Hermione turned out to be the housekeeper: a young and pretty woman who took me to a storeroom on the second floor. "The clothing here is all quite basic," she said, "though certainly well enough made. If I were you I'd go at present for something as simple as jeans and T-shirt and trainers."

Underpants and socks were also supplied and then she left me on my own to change. When I ran back downstairs she was sitting in the manager's office drinking coffee with him. She had poured a cup for me as well. Richard surveyed me in my new garb. "Bit tight across the chest?" he suggested.

"I like a T-shirt tight across the chest." I realized that I was being brazen and hoped I hadn't blushed—but *to thine own self be true*; that's what Brad had many times advised me. "Why else d'you suppose I work out twice a week? *Used* to work out twice a week?"

"Nothing to stop you carrying on with it," Richard observed mildly. "If that's what you have a mind to do."

"Yet you're wanting to say—exhibitionistic. Naff. Aren't you?"

"Not a bit of it," he grinned.

"I get the feeling that you yourself probably work out."

"But I don't pick T-shirts a size too small."

"Is it sinful to be naff?"

"Not altogether cool maybe. But not really any major sin either."

Hermione looked at him and laughed. "Oh come off it Rickie! It's not a sin at all and well you know it." To me she said: "You go with whatever makes you feel right. If you ask me I think you look just fine."

"Oh vanity vanity," said the manager. And gave his head a mournful shake. Reminding me of Brad.

But she seemed pretty much as bolshie as he'd earlier told me I was. "Well even a little bit of that is allowed and don't you try to have us believe otherwise." To accompany those last few words she shook a teaspoon at him.

He made a grimace. "Danny finish your coffee and then we'll get away from this subversive woman." I think he fancied her. I think she fancied him. I suddenly wondered if they were having a relationship.

"Anyway the best of luck," she said to me. "Don't let him bully you."

"I'll try not to. Thank you for your good advice."

"You just remain your own man," she smiled.

"Yep." Yours too I said to Brad. "And Brad's," I told her quite spontaneously.

Richard took me into the dining room . . . with a quick stop-off at the loo. He wanted to order me an early lunch but I felt there was no way I could have handled one. "Anyhow," he said, 'you'll be back here soon enough." So we looked in at the lounge bar. It wasn't full and he stopped to have a short chat with everybody gathered there, some sitting alone, some in couples or groups—his having first, from the doorway, introduced me. Several of the guests offered me wine but I explained I'd only just had coffee. After about a quarter of an hour Richard drew me away. "By now Hermione should have got that package ready."

Since I was anyhow having to visit the hospital they'd decided I might as well carry back as many of the laundered gowns as I could manage; people arrived in them from time to time without there being any settled system for their return. "Yes a bit of a drain on the poor old Health Service," I'd murmured drily.

The parcel proved to be a lot more bulky than anticipated and Hermione worried it could easily grow to be a nuisance over a distance of some two to three miles. I told them I was glad to be of service (asked winningly if this would score me any points); said I could always carry it on my head if necessary and in any case what was the use of going to the gym twice a week if I meant now to be defeated by a silly little bundle of laundry. "Besides," I said, "if I do transport it on my head people will still be able to see my pecs; I feel one has to be considerate regarding all such points as these."

I soon had my comeuppance. Already ten minutes or more into the journey I suddenly realized I had forgotten the raincoat. Ironical or what? I was obliged to go back and collect it. Feeling a bit stupid. Richard saw me off again. "You'd better put it on," he said, "otherwise it will be slipping about all over the place." He not only helped me into it but with a look of benign yet slyly triumphal paternalism insisted on doing up all the buttons while he somehow prevented me from throwing down the bundle and thereby putting up a decent fight.

That raincoat felt practically like a straitjacket.

But I showed a sweet forbearance with him. Because he had shown a sweet forbearance with me.

And of course the moment I was out of sight I attempted to undo the buttons. Yet again—anyway for the time being—there was something which prevented me succeeding.

It was a cheap trick but at least I found it amusing. Not so long ago Brad and I had watched a black-and-white movie made in the Forties. There was one particular line in it which had entered our vocabulary . . . "Okay gov—you got me—it's a fair cop!"

7

AT THE HOSPITAL I left the raincoat precisely where I'd found it but then decided I ought to take that burdensome parcel up to one of the wards and leave it with somebody official; otherwise . . . unattended bags and packages . . . weren't we always being warned to be vigilant? Besides, a very basic amount of explanation would surely be required: "A secondhand stockiest—closing down—wondered whether . . . ?" Or would I then be made to return a second time? Yet it seemed plain I couldn't just stick to the truth, the lovely unvarnished truth. The lovely unvarnished truth could cause nothing but confusion.

I don't know why but I'd thought that perhaps for old times' sake I should go back to the third floor. I took the lift. As I returned down the long corridor I began to sing softly—at first not even realizing I was doing it—telling myself again that he'd be leaving, leaving on that midnight train to Georgia. I was in fact cheerfully acknowledging once more that I'd rather live in his world than live without him in mine when an old woman in a pink nightdress came wandering out of a side ward, grew aware of my presence and appeared to do a double take. She eyed me up and down severely.

"James! So you've decided to come back? And from whose bed *this* time I should like to know!" Her thin grey hair receded at the front but fell almost to her shoulders. Her long and bony nose had a drop quivering at its end. The plunging neckline of her nightie might have seemed better suited to some well-stacked young actress in a sex farce. I said, "I'm sorry but I think you're mistaking me for someone else."

"Oh you think that do you?" One hand shot out and clutched me round the wrist, the fingers gripping with surprising strength. "What have you got in there? All those nastily stained bedsheets you expect me to bung into the wash as usual? Oh Jamie, Jamie! Why must you keep on breaking my heart this way? Why must you? What have I done?"

I looked desperately towards the ward she'd wandered out of, trying to convince myself that at any instant some bustlingly efficient nurse would come rushing forth with cries of humorous reproach: "So there you are me old darlin'. Merciful heavens where are we off to now?" And to me: "Always got an eye out for the boys. She'll have you standing beside her at the altar before you can even say whoops-a-daisy!" I considered calling urgently for aid, not "Help!" exactly but "Excuse me there's a lady come out here . . ." Yet, all the time, she was implacably pushing me back along the corridor and somehow I couldn't find it in me to cry out for assistance. And utterly amazing though it might seem it wasn't actually my own dignity or lack of it that I was thinking about.

"I could better understand it," she said, "if I was being unfaithful too." Her tone had lost its note of accusation; was fast developing into a whine. This was no big improvement. The drop that had been teetering at the tip of her nose now broke away from its anxiously awaiting replacement and, narrowly missing her nightgown, fell neatly between her plimsolls. "Come back to me," she pleaded. "Let's try again to make it work."

What was I to do? Where were all the members of staff? Sod the staff, where were all the patients?

Uncertainty was snatched away from me.

Again I wouldn't quite have used the word 'improvement'.

"Oh," she cried, "oh Christ! Oh James! I'm dying for a shit."

I wildly looked about me. Sweet providence—there was a lavatory nearby; on board that midnight train to Georgia I simply hadn't noticed. "Back there!" I urged. "Look! See the sign?"

She nodded eagerly yet when I tried to pull away continued to hang on. "No, no. Come with me. I can't manage."

"Then it's better if you go on," I said. "I'll send a nurse."

But she was already dragging me forward. "Don't want a nurse! Want you! Oh hurry James I can't hold on!" With her free hand she prodded at the parcel. "Oh drop that stupid thing! Yes I'll wash them for you! Just get me to the lav!"

I dropped the parcel, kicked it to one side. We were almost at the door. I had the feeling I could yet be saved. Some woman washing her hands or combing her hair or applying her lipstick? Yes! Somebody both capable and sympathetic who'd smilingly take charge.

Please.

The room was empty. There was only one cubicle. A notice hung from its door handle. Out of order. Nearest W.C.s attached to the Mary Llewellyn Jenkins ward. The cubicle itself was locked.

"Oh dear Lord!" It erupted from both of us, simultaneously.

"Washbasin!" she said. "Oh help me! Lift me up!" She was already hoicking up her nightdress. "Don't let me do it on the floor."

I took her in my arms and lifted her—she was a greater weight than you'd have thought, I felt the strain in the small of my back—and while I held onto her tightly with one hand tried to keep clear the back of her nightie with the other. Between the two of us we had got her there none too soon. There was a vast bespattering explosion. The pitiful sliver of white soap in its slimy indentation was suddenly shot across with freckles. I felt something dribble down my arm. The smell was powerful to put it mildly. I watched her scrawny mottled legs dangling pathetically over the front of the basin, my arm firmly supporting her so that she didn't sink back into the depths of it; and I said with what I hoped was a nonchalant kind of smile, "There! Does that feel better?"

Yet now she was having a piss, an unexpectedly forceful piss, off which I saw the steam rise. Well count your blessings I told myself. At least this'll help to flush away the gunge.

Not help enough though. That became evident once I'd got her back on the floor. For a minute she just stood there holding up her nightgown, balance a bit uncertain, while I first turned on both taps (however there'd been more pressure in her piss than came from either of those taps or even from the two of them together) then held onto her again while I looked for ways of cleaning off the porcelain. I couldn't come up with any—I saw no kind of brush or sponge or cloth—other than through the direct use of my own right hand. Thankfully the main part of what had come out of her had been quite loose so beneath the sluggish flow of those unwilling taps I smeared my palm and fingers back and forth around the china creating a swirling brown pool that increasingly thinned and lost its density of colour. And left an accumulation of smallish lumps which had to be mashed against the plughole, a process that reminded me of kneading Plasticene or more recently bread dough: frustratingly a skill too late developed, for Brad as well as me. Now somewhat tight-lipped in the energetic employ of my fingertips—for the mashing had become a kind of sieving—I even forgot or else had grown oblivious to the evaporating stench. With both the plughole and the sink again made more or less respectable (and the soap; and my own hand—so far as that sliver without nail-brush could accomplish it) I then ran a deepish pool of warm water and hoisted my now more tractable, less talkative, companion back into her previous position, only this time with her knees pointed a little more towards the ceiling, while I soaped as well as I was able her bottom and vagina and the inside of her thighs, especially at the top. In the absence of any paper towels and feeling unequal for both our sakes to holding her up back and front in close enough proximity to the hot-air machine, even if it worked, I took out the white linen handkerchief with which Hermione had provided me (mightn't there be a good case and not solely on the grounds of economy for the issue of double-strength man-sized tissues; perhaps I ought to mention it?) and dried my new friend off in that rather inadequate fashion. "What's your name?" I asked while I worked at it.

She looked at me uncertainly.

"You're not James are you?"

"No, I'm Danny."

"My parents had a butler called Danny. Or was he the chauffeur? He may have been the chiropodist."

This question exercised us as we made our way out of the small convenience. (Convenience?) At the last moment I noticed there were suspicious brown spots on the lino near the basin but I thought Damn it I've only got my handkerchief; don't the staff in this hospital do *anything*? Besides she needed shepherding, Katy needed shepherding (I'd asked again) back to the ward she'd wandered out of. During our brief walk I retrieved the castigated package and since it was difficult to manage in one hand left her to totter on unaided. Well no not really totter. Without any renewed offer to see to all my washing, not even a patently half-hearted one, she went on ahead at quite a spanking rate and disappeared around the proper door with only one further scrap of communication. "I think he was the chauffeur. He was always very kind to me. Gone but not forgotten. Wish I could remember his name."

I called it after her but felt sure she hadn't heard.

Then I carried on to the Mary Llewellyn Jenkins ward and left the gowns with a sister who was sitting at her desk. I didn't regale her with my little spiel. I merely said, "For the hospital. We hope they'll come in handy. May I use your loo?" She gave me a nice smile, slightly bemused, said, "Thank you. Yes of course," so I knew there was no way they could ever send me back to set *that* particular record straight.

But on my way out I may have bemused her further. "Oh could you tell Katy in the nextdoor ward her chauffeur's name was Danny? Perhaps you could write that down for her?"

Also on my way out I noticed for the first time the little room from which I'd escaped earlier. The door of it was closed. I had no wish at all to see inside.

Fortunately the johns attached to Mary Llewellyn Jenkins were as well-stocked as their brother john was lacking. There was even disinfectant! I smuggled out both this and a J-Cloth and dealt efficiently with the scouring of the basin and the removal of those brown spots from the lino. I then returned the bottle, binned the cloth and made good use of their large green bar of Lifebuoy—plus nailbrush! Gosh did I feel virtuous! During my blessedly unencumbered—and unconstricted—return to Pack Hill I thought Hey bugger me am I going to have a tale to pass on to Richard and Hermione when I put in my request for a surely justified exchange of handkerchief. ("Why what did you do with it?" Rather casually: "Oh . . . you know . . . just happened to dry an old lady's bottom. As you do.") In the meanwhile it was Brad to whom I spoke. "So does that finally answer your question?"

For he had once asked me whether I could imagine looking after him in the most fundamental fashion if he ever happened to catch AIDS or anything else ultimately as incapacitating.

"No," I'd replied. "So please don't include it on any list of things to aim for."

"Then you're saying you don't love me sufficiently to wipe my bum?"

"Not true. What I'm saying is—simply—why do we have to cross our bridges? Of course I could easily enough just give you the answer you're wanting. But until one actually finds oneself in that position . . . ? A bit like being tortured in the war. Sometimes I'm sure I'd have said 'No—please—I'll tell you anything!' no matter how many thousands of lives might have depended on my keeping quiet. But then I think Well perhaps you can't ever be *quite* sure until the contingency arises. Maybe—somehow—from somewhere you do in fact manage to draw the strength. I hope so but I also hope—just as fervently—that I'll never have to find out."

Brad hadn't been impressed. "I see. So you compare wiping my bum to being tortured by the Nazis?"

"Not entirely. But in either case I feel I'd have to close my eyes and think of England."

"I'd wipe your bum like a shot."

"Yes but you're older and wiser not to mention incredibly much nicer. However, just hold on until *I'm* a bit older and wiser and incredibly much nicer, then we can reopen the whole debate. In the meantime when I say I love you as I happen to be saying, you difficult old man, you'll know the sentiment is frightfully well considered; contains nothing of the glib."

It had been bedtime and I remembered only too well the tussle which had followed on from these remarks. "And you have the cheek to call *me* ornery!" I told him now. I laughed and felt exuberant and broke into a run and felt free and wondered what he might be doing at this moment and whether I was filling his thoughts as much as he was filling mine; and as I came to a standstill and wiped the sweat off my face and blew my nose I thought about the possibility of my very shortly catching up with him and launching myself into his arms— and I felt almost unbelievably happy. (Actually it didn't even occur to me that I had blown my nose on an already damp handkerchief; damper than just my sweat alone should have made it. And in retrospect I think I feel glad that this hadn't occurred to me. Poor Katy.) Indeed I could hardly recall a time when I'd felt happier. Not even when he and I had first got together; and that would have taken quite a fair amount of beating.

8

THE PUB WAS CALLED THE CITY OF QUEBEC. It was in a quiet turning off Oxford Street close to Marble Arch. Not simply a gay pub but a known meeting place for older men attracted to younger ones and vice versa. Brad confessed himself bewildered. "I just don't see why young guys should fancy men old enough to be their dads. The other way around of course—no mystery. But in your own case you've still got a father, a father whom apparently you get on well with. So tell me where the attraction lies. I mean in general; I promise I'm not fishing."

I truly couldn't enlighten him.

"You may as well ask why I'm gay as why I go for older men. Or why alone in all my family I'm into westerns and musicals and like vegetable marrow."

"Fair enough," he'd said. "Mine then not to reason why. Mine merely to appreciate and feel happy."

Not that I'd ever viewed Brad as old. When we had met I was twenty-four, he forty-three, but I'd never been the kind of adolescent who thought you were virtually past it at thirty and completely washed up at forty. Besides not only did Brad look fighting fit and youthful, there were men at the Quebec who were well into their seventies, even some who were almost certainly over eighty (not for nothing was the place indulgently referred to as The Elephants' Graveyard), men who even at that age, perplexingly, still attracted lascivious attention and by no means just from the over-fifties . . . or indeed perhaps not at all from the over-fifties; a seventysomething with the arm of a thirty-something draped lovingly around his shoulders was assuredly no uncommon sight even if sometimes—to Brad every bit as much as me—it could begin to verge on the distasteful. But Brad looked like a positive youngster in that sort of assembly and for the two of us to find ourselves drawn to one another wouldn't have seemed in the least unnatural to any of the pub's countless patrons.

I had only been to the Quebec a couple of times and no way would I have gone that evening if I hadn't just survived the final breakup with my current boyfriend. "Well okay I'll show him!" I'd thought. "Plenty of other good fish in the sea." But sitting on the top deck of the No 16 staring out a bit unappreciatively, even blindly, at the charms of Kilburn High Road—I was en route from my bedsit near Cricklewood Broadway—I had no high hopes that the couple of hours ahead were going in any way to lighten my depression; and I very seriously con-sidered dismounting at the next stop and getting drunk at a pub much closer to home. In short it was only my inherent meanness, the fact that I'd already paid my fare, which all too probably prevented me; I was at that time stacking shelves in a supermarket and needing to be careful with my cash, despite a determinedly forgiving and not ungen-erous set of parents. So I stayed on the bus and thought bloody hell what a life and what a total mess I'd made of it and sodding bloody Jonathan could just bloody well sod off and take a running jump. But I was close to crying by this stage so I did try to concentrate at least a little on the life that was being lived in Kilburn.

And in Maida Vale. And along the rest of the Edgware Road. About which not even remotely had it crossed my mind, in primary school in the Midlands, on my first hearing of this noble thoroughfare—and being induced to draw a Roman regiment marching up it stick-limbed to the north—that it would one day provide me with a bus route (southwards) to The City of Quebec. I suppose I couldn't claim to be a prescient child. But now I wondered bleakly if the percentage of gays in Roman times would have been roughly the same as it was today and vaguely envied them their massed ranks; although on the other hand it had never once occurred to me, and surely never would, to sign on in any of Her Majesty's armed forces.

We eventually got to Marble Arch after stopping it seemed at every possible traffic light and every possible request stop. It had begun to rain and of course I hadn't thought to bring my umbrella—I very seldom did, unless it were actually raining when I left home. Therefore I ran and may have reached the pub in something like a minute when normally it would have taken three. As I went in a man was coming out. Our eyes met and held and I was aware of the quickening of my pulse independent of the fact that I'd been running. "Oh hell," smiled the man. "It's raining anyhow. There's just got to be time for another drink. My name's Brad by the way."

As it turned out, there was time for another two drinks (each I mean) and there would certainly have been time for several more—Brad phoned the people he was supposed to be meeting for dinner and asked if they'd forgive him just this once if he cried off. Before that however we had already started to get acquainted.

"I'm assuming Danny," he had said lightly after we had shaken hands, "that you're here on pleasure and not business?"

He was asking more tactfully than others had sometimes asked me in gay bars or clubs whether I was rent; and in fact before my meeting with Jonathan I had occasionally considered such an option—it would have boosted my income no end. But at least sodding bloody Jonathan had saved me from that (he was in many ways a decent bloke; possibly his worst crime lay in being a lot too young for me—he was barely twenty-nine) and for this I must eternally be thankful. I could now hardly believe my wavering self-respect had ever sunk so low.

"Just came in for a drink," I replied, "and to be with other people." Which was the complete truth, apart perhaps from my inaccurate use of the singular. For I hadn't even gone there looking for a pick-up. One-night-stands had never been of much interest. This wasn't to say I sometimes hadn't had them; but only when there'd seemed a good chance of their leading on to something more.

"What will you have?" he asked.

He bought us double Scotches—and not merely Grant's or Bell's but Glenfiddich; it transpired that neither of us had ever been much of a beer-drinker. We sat on one of the red crescent-shaped couches, nylon sprayed with Scotchguard, and under one of those huge purification pipes which were now a feature of the place; and since today was Wednesday and the pub relatively uncrowded we had the couch entirely to ourselves. Behind our heads Shirley Bassey quietly belted out the fact that like Frank Sinatra and innumerable others she did it her way; but after a grimace of resignation from Brad and a responsive but not altogether honest shrug of sympathy from myself we instantly forgot about her. "Do you come here often?" asked Brad. He said it perfectly straight-faced yet even so he got a laugh, brief but spontaneous. "Good," he said. "If you hadn't done that I'd have had to get right up and walk away."

"I don't believe you."

"Oh I'd have taken my drink with me."

"I still don't believe you. And if I did I think I'd be the one who had to get up and walk away. You'd be too frightening. Intolerant. Completely unrelaxable with."

"Is that a word?"

"Certainly. As of this minute anyway."

"And if it wasn't before I don't know how the world ever got on without it."

"I have to admit you don't *seem* too enormously frightening."

"I hope I'm not," he said. "I fear that sometimes I don't suffer fools gladly but that's honestly not something I'm proud of and I'm really doing my damnedest to correct it."

"Tonight?"

"There—and I'd told myself you wouldn't notice!"

"How foolish of you! And I too sometimes fear I don't suffer fools gladly."

"Impasse."

"Isn't it a little soon," I asked, "for strangers to be flirting?" Apparently I already felt quite dangerously at home. I wondered if this was partly an expression of relief. That there could actually be life after Jonathan. Though I knew it was anyway a failing of mine: frequently to come on a bit too strong. I hadn't yet drunk much of my whisky.

"My God! *Which* of us did you suggest was frightening? How old are you Danny?"

I told him.

But like you," I said, "I hope I'm not. Frightening. That's really the last thing in the world I'd want to be. We seem to have a lot in common."

"Tell me about yourself."

"What d'you want to know? Born in a village near Nottingham. My mother a teacher, my father ex-RAF. I've three older brothers and two older sisters who've all settled in various parts of the Midlands. None of them gay. Five nephews and six nieces. Are you finding this fascinating?"

"Yes."

"I'm a big disappointment to my mother and father but nevertheless they love me and I love them. We're a pretty close-knit family all except for me."

"Why should you think you're a disappointment? Because you're gay?"

"Partly that perhaps. But more because I walked out of university in the middle of my course. They feel I'm only half-educated—and the sad thing is they're right."

"What were you reading? And where was it?"

"I was reading Law. At Newcastle. But it was a bad choice of subject. I should have switched."

He waited for me to go on.

"You see, I liked the thought of all that money which solicitors and barristers can rake in. But you can't imagine how dry and dispiriting the actual work was. And when I finally admitted to myself that I was never going to make it—well by then I was just so tired of being with people of my own age. In the main I found them shallow and juvenile even though I was probably equally shallow and juvenile, but in a different way. Have you had enough?"

"No. You give a pretty good impersonation of someone who's a lot more than half-educated."

"Thank you. But that's only bluff."

"I see. So what happened when you left university?"

"I came to London to seek fame and fortune."

"And . . . ?"

"And I'm still working on it. In both departments."

"Fame?" he asked. "As what?"

"Don't laugh. At the start I had some idea of going in for modelling. Or even acting. Remember I was still only nineteen."

"I'm not laughing. Not at all. And now?"

"I think I'd like to write. Steamy adventures of a young gay down from the provinces. Tasting life in the big city."

"And planning to remain?"

"Oh very much so. Didn't someone once say that if you're tired of London you must be tired of life?"

"Yes good old Doctor Johnson. But that was before traffic pollution and mobile telephones and—I think—Miss Shirley Bassey." (Here I ought to say that Miss Bassey had long since been replaced by Liza Minnelli and Abba, several songs from Abba, and now by another lady—"Jerry Sothern," said Brad—who was plaintively asking if she'd recognize the light in his eyes/ which no other eyes reveal/ or shall I pass him by/ and never realize/ that he was my . . . ideal? For some reason the wistful quality of the singer's voice or the poignancy of the lyric itself, with all its emphasis on—according to Brad—the haphazardness of fate, had briefly attracted the attention of us both.) "This young gay down from the provinces though: how does he manage to get by?"

"He stacks the shelves at Price-As-You-Like-It. In Cricklewood Lane."

"Ah. And I'm sure it doesn't get much steamier than that." He nodded towards my nearly empty glass. "Same again?"

"This time it has to be my turn."

But he was already on his feet. "Let's wait until that novel of yours hits the bestseller lists."

"Brad I didn't say it was a novel." (Though it was of course.) "I suspect you have this fearful habit of jumping to conclusions."

He laughed. "Your own personal adventures then? Less truthful than fiction yet far more imaginative. Come on—tell me I sound like a very poor imitation of Oscar Wilde."

"Oh I wouldn't be so impolite. Why would you accuse me of being that?"

"Maybe because I jump to conclusions; and maybe because I get the feeling you're someone who would, almost automatically, keep a person on his toes."

"Quite frightening in fact?"

"No. I think I'd be more inclined to call it . . ."

But the right word didn't come to him immediately; and whilst he was searching for it I swiftly rose and preceded him to the bar. The thing was I didn't want him to believe I was simply on the take . . . even if at least to some extent I knew I was. (The proper study of mankind is man was something else I remembered somebody had once said.) We had been talking for longer than it might appear and Brad had already paid for our first two rounds; at least I had sufficient money to buy a couple of Glenfiddichs and still with any luck have bus fare home. (He mustn't think that I was going to be too easy. I had no intention of letting him get me into bed that night.)

Yet he caught up with me well before I had a chance to place my order. ". . . bracing," he informed me with a grin. "Look. It's getting late and I haven't eaten yet. What about you? Let's transfer this meeting to a restaurant."

"I had a sandwich earlier—"

"A growing boy needs more than just a sandwich."

A growing boy did. And anyway that sandwich now seemed a long time ago: before Jonathan had unexpectedly turned up in what was clearly confrontational mood. (Me, I was never confrontational.) I said: "I'll have to find a cashpoint."

"No you won't," said Brad.

Which was absolutely just as well. Having found a cashpoint I could have done little more than merely wink at it and ask it how it did.

It was then he made his phone call.

"A *mobile*?" I said. "Really? Earlier on I must definitely have misunderstood something. Well, well."

"I only use it for emergencies," he told me drily. "Never for quite unnecessary chats."

"Yes of course. Naturally. Emergencies . . ." I said. "Yes."

We went to a small French restaurant in a backstreet on the other side of Edgware Road. Brad apologized for its being a little twee—the curtains, tablecloths and napkins were all in different shades of pink although the rest of the clientele were of both sexes and appeared to be quite straight—but he said the cooking was good and he ordered us a delicious meal. At least I have a vague impression of its being a delicious meal but I truly (and very regrettably) wasn't paying it much attention. I had told him during our fifteen-minute walk, mostly unrained-on, that this time the spotlight would be trained exclusively on him.

"But I'm not sure I want to be under any spotlight." This protest came soon after we'd been seated at a table beneath a reproduction of Édouard Manet's *Le Déjeuner Sur L'Herbe*—so I'd been informed when I had briefly shown an interest.

"Well now that is tough," I sympathized. "I really am sorry."

"On the other hand I'm always happy to have one fairly nearby. A spotlight."

"Meaning what? That you enjoy the theatre?"

"Yes!" He seemed pleased. "And I write for it as well."

"Really? You're a playwright?"

He nodded.

"And you mean that you've had your plays produced? Here in London? In the West End?"

"And on Broadway. And in thirty capitals or more around the world, including Peking and Tokyo. And not just the capitals. And on the road in America and Canada. And in lots of cities over here—including both Nottingham *and* Newcastle. Not to mention seaside theatre in the summer and amateur productions throughout the year."

"Christ! You're well-known."

"And you must want to say bigheaded."

"I'm sorry I didn't recognize your name."

"That's all right. You couldn't place Johnson's either."

"But at least I saw *Volpone* when I was still at school." I saw him smile a little but he said nothing. "I might just as easily have seen one of your plays. How many are there? Tell me the names of some."

"Not all?"

"No that isn't fair: I'm the one with a reputation for keeping people on their toes! But naturally that's what I meant. Are they exciting and tender and very serious?"

"And do they explore weighty contemporary issues? Yes. About to the same degree I'd say as *Charley's Aunt*."

He then quite leisurely ticked off a list of titles; he'd told me there were nine. I wanted to say Yes I've seen that—I've seen that—I've seen that; but no way was it possible; the theatre hadn't played much part in my experience up till then. What I could say was, "*Where Two Roads Meet*—wasn't there a film called that?" Even as I did so this struck me as a bit tactless but I wanted to come up with something knowledge-able and indicative of interest and as relevant as I could manage.

"Yes," he said, "that was mine."

"But . . . ?"

"But what?"

"Wasn't it American . . . and big budget . . . and starring some really top names?" Yet annoyingly, try as I might, I couldn't bring to mind which top names.

"Yes but all the same it wasn't very good."

"God I wish I'd seen it though!"

"It's done on DVD."

I was no longer even thinking about playing hard to get although perhaps there was now more reason why I should have been.

"And did you meet them, all those famous stars?"

Thereafter for the next half-hour or so our conversation was entirely movie stuff—American *and* British—because he'd also had a play made into a film over here. *Daisy and Sybella*. That too was out on video.

"I want to see them both!"

"Well I reckon that could be arranged," he said. "Only not tonight—not tonight!"

Why not tonight? My first flicker of doubt. Didn't he fancy me as much as I'd assumed?

Uncertainty of course increased not only his attractiveness but my own determination.

"Are you writing anything at present?"

"There's a new one about to go into rehearsal."

"With a thumping big part in it for me?"

"Telepathy! I'd been on the very point of saying keep all your evenings free in anticipation of a long run."

And *I'd* been on the very point of saying: But will you take me to the first night? By then I had inside me in addition to two double whiskies a glass and a half of red wine—all of it being mulled by my heady imaginings of the life he led and by my awareness of some of the people he had met. There'd also been the Cointreau with my coffee. By then too—even though he'd decided for some reason to pay by credit card—I'd caught a glimpse of his plentifully filled wallet. Scarcely necessary indeed, not from the beginning: his shirt, pullover, trousers, shoes—all of them proclaimed Armani; none of them Marks & Spencer. Even had he been dressed in nothing but swimming trunks there would still have been an air of dealing only at the best places. The way he was groomed: the haircut, the cologne, the smoothness of his shaven skin; his hands, his wristwatch—the way that he behaved: his confidence, the casual ordering of Glenfiddich. To place him in a rich man's world I'd clearly had no need to hear about his plays and films; but at the same time they'd added a beguiling new dimension. And for the moment I thought I had his interest. Despite the whisky and the wine and the liqueur I struggled once again to keep him at a distance. I made no mention of the first night and even pretended to have to smother a yawn.

"God! I'm sorry. I suddenly feel so tired. If you're not going to give me the lead role in your play I think I should be making tracks for home." It was now getting on for twelve.

I noticed again the way his wrists looked. Perhaps absurdly this made me feel a little better about myself. I remembered that I'd already found him physically attractive the first moment I had seen him and that I'd already been responding to his personality very early on in our acquaintance; would have liked him just as much if I hadn't guessed the condition of his bank balance and if he'd only bought me two singles of Grant's. Surely?

"I'll be picking up a taxi," he said. "I can drop you off."

"Of course. Cricklewood's in a direct line to Holland Park. By far the shortest route."

"I'd be glad of the extra ten minutes of your company."

"Then give me a ring next week or whenever you're free and I'll give you ten times ten minutes of my company. Or even more if you feel that you can stand it. I'll take you to a greasy spoon and lead you step by step into such infinite mysteries as the methods of stock control at Price-As-You-Like-It. Plus the lowdown on all the romance that springs up in the checkout queues. Could maybe provide you with the plot for your next play. Forget the *Price* and you've even got a good title."

We shook hands before I saw him into his taxi and shut the door on him. It was a long and firm and meaningful handshake (and not far off electric). As the taxi moved away he turned and waved. I liked that; I had always liked people who waved. I didn't take the bus, I suddenly wanted to walk. After some forty minutes when I was two-thirds of the way home it came on to rain again. Quite heavily. I didn't mind. In fact I was wearing only a shirt above my jeans and I unbuttoned this right down to my belt. I got drenched and fairly revelled in it. I sang 'Singin' in the Rain' and several other things not at all connected with the weather. I felt wonderful. I had the shrewdest suspicion even then that I'd just met the man who was going to change my life.

9

I DIDN'T TELL RICHARD OR HERMIONE a single thing about my adventure with Katy—not in the end. Thinking about Brad as I walked back up Pack Hill (as when wasn't I thinking about Brad? It was like the first weeks of our being in love. No, months. Had I ever really stopped?), thinking about those very early days of our friendship/courtship/romance—whatever the proper expression is—I suddenly remembered a time when sauntering along in the sunshine to Leicester Square, a little early for our date, I had caught sight of him in the crowds a bit further on and had naturally broken into a run. But before I reached him he'd begun speaking to a boy of about sixteen who was sitting on the pavement outside an amusement arcade with his back against the wall and a piece of cardboard in his lap: "Hungry and homeless." Coming to a stop nearby I saw Brad squat down, obviously to talk more easily, then hand the lad a banknote—or what might have been several banknotes—and even more remarkably hand him something else he'd just extracted from his wallet: his business card no less, a brother to the one he'd given me outside the restaurant on our first night. Then after glancing at his watch Brad rose from his haunches and shook the boy's hand.

He headed again towards the Odeon but turned and waved briefly (he waves to all of us I thought). The boy was gazing after him with a rapt expression on his foxy pockmarked face—the 'foxy' could be subjective, I simply had no sympathy for losers—yet didn't acknowledge the wave. I made a quick but effective detour then hurried after Brad. "Are you crazy?" I asked without preamble, without even the least attempt at greeting.

"Why? What's the matter?" None too surprisingly he seemed rather taken aback. We stood outside the entrance to the cinema.

"What's the matter? Only that you'll end up with a knife between the shoulder blades—that's what's the matter—or a robbed and vandalized apartment! Or at the very least a non-stop string of beggars at your front door! *That* is what's the matter!"

"Oh! You mean that boy just now . . . ?"

I'd at sometime read or heard that adults didn't blush or, if there were to be exceptions, only those with the lightest colouring and the fairest skin. But Brad blushed. He most definitely did blush.

"My God!" I said. "You couldn't possibly have thought him pretty?"

"No of course not. What is this? What's got into you?"

"Are you in the habit of handing out your card to all and sundry?"

"I warn you: this is a conversation I'm not enjoying. So shall we put an end to it and go in and see this wretched film you want to see?"

"You would never have told me would you? If I hadn't happened to come along at the exact right moment?"

"Told you what precisely? And no. Why should I have?"

I was almost shaking in my anger; my humiliation. I hadn't yet been to his flat, two DVDs to be watched or no, because I'd known full well what would happen the first time I walked into it—my own lack of resolve as much as his—and I'd wanted to delay that scene as long as possible: partly because I really enjoyed being courted (while feeling confident of the eventual outcome) yet even more of course because I'd aimed to keep him keen. But I was naïve. It had never occurred to me that I was simply one in a long line of pick-ups; that sixteen-year-olds on the street were being invited to precede me, follow me, or, if they chanced to turn up at an opportune instant, conceivably join in. Copies of that card were probably circulating all over London. "Damn it!" I cried—and in fact 'cried' was the right word, my voice had broken on a sob. "Damn it, I thought that I was special."

This time it was him who caught me up.

"Danny cool down," he said. "Cool down. There's normally such a thing as a trial, you know, before the verdict is returned." He was still angry but at least he was remaining calm. There might have been embarrassment along with the anger: a number of people were turning to stare at us, one or two even stopping, and there was nothing furtive about their interest. "Don't you want to hear the case for the defence?" He smiled ironically; having partly addressed this question to the passersby—or non-passersby. Successfully. It shamed them into movement.

I stared blindly at the pavement.

"What defence? You've already admitted you wouldn't have told me. It's only because you were caught at it red-handed."

"Oh yes? Caught at what?"

"At bribing and soliciting."

"My God! You really are a filthy-minded little pervert!"

And it should have been funny—believe me it wasn't—it was now he who turned upon his heel.

I stayed there motionless for up to a full minute. Still just staring at the ground. I felt numbed, I felt icy, I felt (equally as contradictory) that if anyone bumped into me or stopped to ask me if I was all right it would be enough to set me howling, howling uncontrollably, there in full view. I dragged myself to a bench inside the garden in the middle of the square. A woman and her small daughter were sitting at the other end, companionably reviewing their purchases. I wasn't surprised when they shortly moved away; no one feels comfortable alongside glassy-eyed dejection. I didn't know how *I* was ever going to find the energy to move away. Not until they came to lock the gates at any rate. There just didn't seem the slightest point. Where was I to go?

This was my day off. In lieu of last Sunday. It would have been our fourth outing. Our fourth outing in slightly under two weeks. Our first time at a cinema. I'd been wondering if we might hold hands.

I had taken the bus to Oxford Circus, walked leisurely down Regent Street. It was one of those times when I'd been resolving yet again to appreciate each passing minute as fully as I could. We'd probably have been spending some eight or nine hours together; by far the longest period yet. A full five hundred of those passing minutes. I'd felt rich and didn't mean to squander.

And now . . . nothing. Over. All those dreams of the past fortnight, all those dreams and largely sleepless nights, all those first waking thoughts, all that doubt, those endless replays and those reassuring phone calls, all that fluctuating happiness, that wondrous worrying obsession: concern for someone else's safety like you never felt concern about your own. All of it now gone. Over. (Except for the obsession and the sleepless nights.) A total waste of emotion and energy and time.

Totally draining.

And life had never seemed so empty.

Nor expendable.

It must have been the worst hour that I'd ever spent. It felt more like two or even three. I was in hell. And there was no way out; nowhere to go. Could I ever return to my room—in which I'd been so happy when I'd last seen it? To my colleagues at the shop—towards whom I had been feeling so unusually well-disposed when I had last wished them all goodnight? Indeed, to anything I had ever known before the destruction of this eagerly anticipated afternoon?

"Come on it can't be quite as bad as that." He put his arm around my shoulders. I'd hardly registered that anyone at all had sat beside me. Let alone who.

I had foreseen that I would howl the very moment I was touched. Great racking sobs. Even the notion of my fine and manly beauty being so seriously impaired—not to mention the notion of my fine and manly street cred—couldn't in any way prevent it. I laid my head against his chest. There went *his* fine and manly street cred too. It didn't seem to faze him.

"I'll tell you why I wasn't going to speak of it," he said. This was after I'd managed to compose myself, had sat up, wiped my eyes, blown my nose and tried to smooth away the damp creases at the front and centre of his shirt. "Nothing was further from my mind than soliciting. I don't in the least bit fancy kids, not even when they're manifestly clean, not even when they're all dewy-eyed and appealing. What I was trying to do was—well merely offer help. Apparently they don't get any of it from the state, boys and girls as young as that."

He hesitated.

"Of course it would have been so easy just to give him money and then walk off feeling virtuous as if I'd actually put myself out in some way, made the world a better place. But Danny I ask you: what real good would it have done? Bought him a meal perhaps, a drink, a fix, a pathetically short-lived period of escape. That isn't any sort of answer. Is it?"

He pursed his lips. I still didn't say anything.

"So I gave him my card. And if he follows up on it, as I very much hope he will, I'll try to provide not simply short-term comfort—bed, bath, food, TV—but also the best professional treatment going. Counselling. Rehabilitation. I can afford to pay for things like that. How could I live with myself if I merely went to first nights and premières, travelled and bought pictures? And it may be slightly risky as you say but isn't the whole of life to some degree a gamble and don't we almost need to take risks? And as yet I haven't ended up with any knife between the shoulder blades."

I said: "If that was all"—all?—"I still don't understand why you tried so hard to keep it from me."

"Because I do so little good in this world—possible good I should say, one's never sure how things are going to turn out—that on the rare occasions when it does happen . . . well the last thing I'm after is to advertise. Obviously. The overall impression people got would be so hopelessly far from the truth."

"All right," I said. "So your wicked little secret is simply this? That you're either already a saint or at some stage are going to become one?"

"You see? The perfect Illustration! My point exactly. However!" He smiled. "Are we still friends?"

I felt impelled to tell the truth.

"Brad when I saw you give that card—before I came running over to harangue you like a fishwife—I went across and snatched it back." Without looking at him I leant over and took the small crumpled thing out of the rear pocket of my jeans. "I did it to protect you. As I thought."

That wasn't the whole truth; but at least it was a large part of it.

He said, "Then will you take it back. And apologize."

"Oh God. Must I?"

"Please?"

Amazingly the boy was still there.. Why hadn't he gone leaping off to celebrate his windfall? He looked just as blank when I returned the card as he had when I had snatched it from him.

Perhaps he was so stoned he didn't remember me.

"Sorry," I mumbled. "I had no right." And then, scared he hadn't heard, I repeated this more loudly. I dipped into my pocket, gave him all the change in it, luckily only a pound coin, a twenty-pence piece and some pennies (not that I thought he either needed or deserved it), taking good care as I did so not to touch contaminating fingers. Wondered if Brad had come to the entrance of the garden; might be watching.

He was still where I had left him, facing the shiny black bulk of the Odeon. (But perhaps, neck swivelled, he could still have seen from there?) "Thank you for that," he said. "And thank you for wanting to protect me. I'd like you to realize I appreciate the thought."

"So *are* we still friends?"

"Maybe better than ever. Yes?"

That was the first time we had kissed—full on the lips albeit very briefly—and right in the middle of Leicester Square in broad daylight in the very heart of London's tourist-thronged West End. Under the watchful though inscrutable eye of William Shakespeare; under the watchful though inscrutable eye of Charlie Chaplin too.

"And is it really a wretched film?" I said. "And is it true it's only me, not you, who wants to see it?"

"I'll tell you what: *you* could practise being a little more saintly—if part of that means not referring to the very foolish things a person may come up with in the heat of the moment."

Anyway. I didn't tell Richard or Hermione about Katy.

(And soon, indeed, couldn't have told them about her. My memory of the whole experience grew as hazy as a dream. I've seldom been good at reliving my dreams.)

So you see Brad what a shining influence you are. And always have been. My God, Judgment Day for you should be a doddle—I mean if you were being accurately assessed as you went along as I hope and imagine that you were. Despite all the crap you handed out about the falsity of overall impressions.

No wonder you didn't have to hang around.

The only thing is now: how the bloody hell am I myself ever going to manage? You in, me out. I don't think I could endure that any more than the other way about—or certainly not *much* more; I'm clearly still as selfish as I've ever been, notwithstanding your excellent example. Somehow you're going to have to pull me through, show how conniving you can be as well as merely good. Otherwise I start to feel I haven't got a chance.

10

I HAD A LATE LUNCH. A late lunch with my late grandmother. Of course I kept forgetting that I myself was late. I also kept forgetting that Isabella—she repeatedly asked me to call her Isabella—was my grandmother. Not altogether surprising. She looked thirty-five.

We sat alone in the dining room at a table by the window with that view across the Downs to the Channel. Richard hadn't introduced us or even told me I'd see anyone I knew. He'd simply sent me in to get some lunch and she'd got up from the table and advanced smilingly to meet me. And the strange thing is I'd known who she was. Even before she'd said anything.

Halfway across the room she came to a halt and held her arms out.

"Hello my love. And welcome—welcome! Can you believe it: you were fifteen when I saw you last? It feels like yesterday!"

She didn't exactly talk like a twenty- or thirtysomething. But then neither did she talk much like the eightysomething I had chiefly known.

"And just look at you now! Didn't I always say you'd leave a trail of broken hearts?"

I did remember that she'd said it once. I suppose it hadn't *always* been a case of reprimands and negatives. But in the past I would never have described her as a gusher. Never.

She threw her arms about me and kissed me warmly on both cheeks.

"Though in my great unworldliness I think I vaguely assumed those hearts would all be female!"

No, definitely. This was not the grandmother I had thought I knew. This was a grandmother I might really have cried about when they told me she was dead.

"Oh Lord!"

"What is it dear?"

"Does that mean everyone's aware I'm gay?"

She laughed and took my hand and led me back to the table; but didn't attempt to answer that question until we were settled and had our napkins in our laps and had started on our soup.

"Well yes I suppose it does—anyone, I mean, who's been interested and looking out for you. But they don't give that much for it!" She snapped her fingers; I'm sure in life I'd never seen her snap her fingers.

I said: "I'm sorry that I didn't cry at your funeral."

"Oh for heaven's sake! *I* wouldn't have cried at my funeral. And whatever else you have or haven't been young Danny at least you were never a hypocrite."

"And I'm sorry that I used to mimic you."

"I'm not. You gave us lots of laughs. I always said you'd have a future on the stage."

"Clearly I didn't know you."

"Who did? Who did? Other of course than those who'd gone ahead and were busy keeping tabs on *me*."

"Yes that's what's worrying. That's why I said Oh Lord."

"You mean were we hot on your tail each time you went into the lavatory? Or at bedtime? Or quite often not at bedtime and not even in the bedroom?"

"Something like that—yes."

"What can I say? I'm sure you'll soon find out yourself. We're not *voyeurs*; I'd call us interested observers of the human heart and human condition. And intensely sympathetic ones. We may sometimes laugh a little at the sheer absurdity of so much of it—people's lives seem just so *serious* to themselves don't you know—but the laughter will never be unkind; we've all been there ourselves, remember, we were all a part of it."

As she said that, Hermione arrived with the omelettes and salad which we'd asked for, and with the bottle of white wine. All of them—they were the best I'd ever tasted; just like the soup had been. But I could so easily have got distracted from the quality of both the food and the wine. My grandmother had unexpectedly become grave.

"Darling, although the human *condition* is the phrase I may have used I want you to understand I've been prattling on only about the human *comedy*. Obviously there are many times when people can't laugh at all, not remotely, and then the only thing they *can* do is call upon the rest of us—or anyway a large enough group of us—to back them in their prayers and tell them it's all right to shake their fists in fury."

She continued in this far more sober vein. Only a short while later she told me about the wholesale grief of my parents and family. While relating it she didn't sound judgmental and yet I guessed something of what lay beneath her neutral tone, and had the grace for the first time since roughly half-past-eight that morning to feel seriously shaken by the thing I'd done. But then I reminded myself (defiantly) that my parents still had themselves and five other children to invest their futures in while Brad and I merely had each other. Nevertheless—with Isabella's keen participation—I offered up a short but fervent prayer both for my own parents and for Brad's. Also for the rest of our respective families. Then for myself as well. I asked them to forgive me.

After that we spoke of my immediate future.

"Do I get to have a say in it?"

"Oh yes. Make any suggestion you feel you'd like to."

"Only one suggestion. That I be allowed to catch up with Brad. And fast!"

"Now how did I know you were going to say that?"

But I didn't return her smile. I felt sure it was about to be followed by a negative.

"Though I'm afraid it isn't that straightforward."

"Why not?"

"Because."

Now with just one word she did sound a little more like the grandmother I remembered. She had said it half-humorously but her humour had misfired. She must have sensed this.

"Darling I'm sorry. But there are some things you simply can't be permitted to know yet. And one of those is why Brad was moved on from here before you yourself arrived."

"Had they let him know I was arriving?"

I think the urgency in my tone was what made her put down her spoon—we were by then eating our ice cream—what made her briefly touch my hand.

"Believe me if I could tell you I would."

So they hadn't let him know. For, if they had, no way could he have been prevailed upon to leave. I felt both cheated by what I was picking up and reassured by it.

"Now to get back to the future," said Isabella, "the immediate future, this is how it's going to be." She had withdrawn her hand and suddenly seemed more businesslike. "When the day of your funeral arrives—and, I have to warn you, time in The Halfway House appears almost to be telescoped—it wouldn't be a bad idea for you to go to the reception . . . or wake or whatever you want to call it. Invisibly of course. And in the meanwhile you can just spend a very peaceful time resting here and walking in the gardens: generally recharging your batteries and mulling things over. Think of this as being the perfect place for a retreat."

"In other words somewhere for me to twiddle my thumbs and kick my heels?"

"Or in still other words my darling"—she smiled at me sweetly— "to make the very most of a spot of enforced idleness."

"But can't you see this is just the time I need to be *doing* things? Moving forward? Getting rid of my frustrations?" Yes 'retreat' summed it up all right; I wanted to advance, to be pressing onwards and upwards, *per ardua ad astra*. It might have been different if I was old and worn out—I could appreciate that. But I was young and energetic; and that's what they were failing to understand, they the powers that be. I tried to put this into words but Isabella gently overrode me.

"And you can read books and watch television," she said—my grandmother the arch-temptress; she must have been attending workshops run by Eve. "Just regard it as a mini-break, a bonus, an unexpected chance to recharge."

Again. I didn't need to recharge. I needed to charge. "Television?" I repeated. On a note of disbelief.

"The Fantasy Channel."

"Oh great! Wizards and witches and dragons! Just what I always dreamed of: to go to heaven and hope to meet a few wizards and witches and dragons on the way." But at least I smiled a little as I said it. I wasn't being totally curmudgeonly—I mean not *totally*.

"Wizards and witches and dragons? Oh my love! No it isn't like that at all."

She explained to me then what it was like. In the right mood I might have found it more seductive.

It seemed that on the Fantasy Channel I could become the strongest man in the world if I felt like it, or the cleverest, or the richest; I could become the greatest lover, the best tennis player; yachtsman, golfer, fencer, skater—jockey—well you only have to name it, the possibilities appeared to be endless.

I could star with Leonardo DiCaprio, Brendan Fraser, Brad Pitt— whoever—and still be assured of top billing.

I could make love to Ingrid Bergman in *Casablanca* if I wanted. I could make love to Humphrey Bogart in *Casablanca* if I wanted.

Like that lyric in *A Chorus Line* had put it, I could dig right down to the bottom of my soul and just see what the screenwriter in residence came up with. It could be fun. It could be magical. It could be Hollywood at its most richly glamorous and its most extravagantly escapist.

Brad *Pitt*? Hell no. What was I thinking of? I could direct and co-star with his namesake: a feel-good movie par excellence equipped with a quite shamelessly romantic ending.

Yet hold on a tick. Escapist? That meant, didn't it, you came out of *The Sound of Music* or *My Fair Lady* or *An American in Paris* and woke up to the fact it was five o'clock on a cold wet evening in the suburbs and there was a note on the table telling you to get your own tea since everybody else would be back late; and you found the cat had spewed up copiously across the kitchen floor?

So maybe it was better to try to temper the escapist bit. I didn't want to return into a world where it was a cold wet evening in the suburbs—dark too—and people jostled you with their umbrellas and seemed thoroughly bad-tempered and it came back with a jolt that Brad wasn't with you nor was he anywhere around.

Nothing too feel-good therefore. No. Though I wasn't quite sure what that left.

11

I THOUGHT AT FIRST that I might get to be John Wayne (perhaps circa the time of *Stagecoach*) and in a typical John Wayne movie.

But . . .

It was a small square cell from which through the bars I could see my jailer—the sheriff—leaning comfortably back in his chair with both boots on the desk and a straw stuck in his mouth.

"Though why am I here?" I was the only prisoner. I spoke from my hard cot in a dark corner.

The sheriff removed the straw from between his yellowed teeth and after a moment's amassing preparation spat into a nearby receptacle which was clearly made of metal—we heard a small but self-important clang.

He was an old man: weather-beaten and grizzled and ruminative.

"Aw," he said. "That's for you to say." Back went the straw.

"What?"

He plainly didn't feel it had to be repeated.

"I mean—what have I been charged with?" I tried to think back. I wondered whether it was something to do with gambling; perhaps I'd been drunk; perhaps I'd been in some whorehouse or saloon where quarrels got picked—and fast guns drawn—all on the turn of a questionable quicksilver card.

"Aw." Apparently repetition now became acceptable. "That's for you to say."

He was obviously a simpleton. I hadn't much patience with simpletons.

"Oh for heaven's sake! Don't you know, man?"

"Nope."

"Isn't it your business to find out?"

"Nope."

"Who brought me in?"

"Found you here this morning. Keys back on desk. Shucks. Often seems to happen that way."

He smiled companionably; pondering life's little mysteries.

"How long do I have to stay?"

"Well I suppose that depends," he nodded.

"On what?"

"How long it takes you. Shoot! How should I know?"

I wasn't sure if I could stand much more of this. I had to keep stomach-clenchingly quiet for an instant while I tried to control my irritation. "How long it takes me to do what?"

"Work out what you're charged with. Then what you ought to do about it. Then if you feel prepared to go ahead and do it. You ready for some grub yet?"

"No." After a pause I grudgingly softened it. "Thanks." Hardly his fault he was such a dunderhead. I sat on my cot and drew up my knees; encircled them with my arms. Went on trying to remember. I might have been drinking but at least I had no hangover. My brain seemed clear. Was I a cardsharp? Con man? Killer? Thief?

I wasn't a killer. They'd hardly have bothered with the jail. They'd have strung me up on the spot. They? The good citizens of this plainly one-horse town. Besides. If you'd killed someone you'd know about it, you'd have to know about it. My instincts told me I couldn't be a killer. Hadn't got the guts.

No—be fair to yourself—that wasn't the reason.

Thief?

No.

Oh yes sometimes when I'd thought I could get away with it I'd travelled on the train without a ticket and when I'd transported my TV set from home to Cricklewood I hadn't taken out a licence but I don't think I'd ever actually stolen from anyone, not even as a kid, not even later on from Price-As-You-Like-It when small amounts of pilfering were regarded almost as a part of one's wage; and if I'd ever found anything of value in the street I'd immediately taken it to a police station. My parents had raised me to be honest.

Con man then? Well only in the sense we all were. We tried to look confident when we weren't, we projected an image, embroidered an anecdote: usually stories which redounded (ever so subtly) to our own credit. But I had never tried to take anybody in with mischievous intent, and the lies I'd told had only been the kind that made life easier for everyone. Again. My parents had aimed to make us all considerate.

But still—

"What's your name?" I asked.

"Clem."

Well wouldn't you just have known it: that his name would almost have to be Clem?

"I'm Danny. Clem? Were *you* brought up to be considerate?"

"What kid ain't if he's raised up in a good home?"

"And were you raised up to be charitable?"

"How d'ya mean? Money to the poor and sichlike?"

"No I guess I'm thinking more about attitude: attitude towards the poor and suchlike. Giving money to them is the easy part." Oh yeah? I was remembering that afternoon in Leicester Square—well naturally I was. "Not that I ever did. Give them much. Always told myself I couldn't afford to. Another time maybe; when things got easier."

When things got easier . . . But even with Brad I'd tried as far as possible to contribute to household expenses; hadn't aimed to be a kept man. My salary from The White Hart had mainly been spent, if not on necessities or keeping myself looking decent (though Brad had always paid our fees at the gym), then on various bits and pieces I'd hoped were going to give him pleasure.

He'd probably have preferred me to spend it on the poor.

The sheriff spat again; again there was a clearly relished sound effect.

"Can't say I ever thought a whole heap about it," he remarked after a moment. "Can you be reared to feel them proper things you should towards the poor?"

I didn't see why not. Superficially at any rate. But how deep it was going to permeate plainly depended a great deal less on your parents and a great deal more on yourself. And the sad thing was for me—I had to face up to this—it so clearly hadn't taken.

"With me it didn't take," I said.

"Don't follow you too well."

"Who would?" I struggled to explain it; for both our sakes. "I think I never walked a mile in another man's shoes, never more than a yard or two at most. I think I never said, 'There but for the grace of God . . .' Not seriously that is, not more than as a thing to say. I suppose in fact I didn't waste much time in thinking about them at all—the really poor, the dispossessed—other than as total losers who in the long term had only themselves to blame. I think more than anything I usually felt revulsion and contempt. No that isn't true: more than *anything* I usually felt indifference."

"And is this then the charge you're considering of?"

"I suppose it is—basically. Because that's what I had on my own doorstep and could have tried to do something about." I paused. "Though of course it reached out way beyond the poor on my own doorstep."

"You're doing well Dan I reckon you're doing well. I guess you'll be out of here in no time."

I hadn't been setting out to impress him nor expecting either encouragement or understanding from such a seemingly unlikely quarter. So to add to all my other sins I was patently a patronizing git. I smiled a little bleakly. "Thank you for your sympathy. You should have been a priest." I looked about me at my tiny cell. "This should have been the confessional."

He gave his yellow gap-toothed grin and meditatively—raspingly—rubbed his leathery unshaven chin. "But you always did show a fondness for them old western movies. Din't you boy?"

Yes especially for the ones so old they were frequently in black-and-white. Where the good guys had invariably won and the bad guys had invariably received their just deserts. A fairy tale for all ages: monochrome simplicity. Why couldn't life itself have been like that?

But if it had been . . . if it had been . . . ? The question then was this. Would old Danny Boy have emerged wholeheartedly on the side of the marshal and the homesteaders? Or might he have been one of those outlaws weakly swayed by the rationalizations of a greedy and uncaring boss?

Because—yes—the indifference had reached way out. Dramatically. Victims of earthquake, flood and cyclone. Victims of war and civil war and genocide. Of terrorism. Victims of murder and torture and mutilation. Had I ever really *cared*? (Apart from New York and London, that is, but they of course were easy.) Often plenty of lip service naturally—maybe a reaction of genuine abhorrence lasting *a full five minutes* before the sigh and the switching of the channels and the pouring of the glass of Scotch. But could you really be raised to feel more than that . . . just that very fleeting moment of compassion? No man is an island. Any man's death diminishes me. Because I am involved in mankind.

John Donne was Brad's favourite poet. I'm not sure I'd even heard of him before I met Brad. I do know I could never have recited a single line of his entire output.

And therefore never send to know for whom the bell tolls; it tolls for thee.

I wish I could have written that. I mean I wish I could have written that in the knowledge of its being an absolutely honest reflection of the way I felt.

"He lacked compassion Clem."

"Who did?"

"That's what they should have written on my tombstone. Or"—once more I had forgotten—"should be about to write on it. I think that sums it up."

In fact I had usually been more moved by the agony of just one individual. Only look at that girl of fifteen who had been killed by over fifty knife wounds slowly inflicted by her boyfriend. Or at the young man who had been kicked to death by three assailants in the street—every bone in his head had been broken. Or at families, often children, who awoke to find their homes on fire and themselves most terrifyingly trapped.

Or think about Ken Bigley. Imprisoned for weeks and growing old and growing thin from anticipating his threatened end—decapitation. And think about his eleventh-hour escape from the house, his stumbling flight across the field at its rear, his no doubt burgeoning hope of deliverance. Think about his sudden awareness that he had been spotted; that his jailers were fast catching up on him. Whilst brandishing their implement of execution. Only think about it.

Or think about James Bulger, the three-year-old plastered in model paint and then stoned to death, his body left on the railway line, to be cut in half by an early-morning goods train.

Or think about anyone, absolutely anyone, who'd had the misfortune to die horrifically. Where *was* God, on all occasions such as these?

(Yet nobody ever asked where was God when all the good things happened: when the universe was created, the first breath of human life blown into it—animal life as well—when butterfly wings began to be designed.)

But even after learning of these sorts of tragedy how long-lasting had been my state of sober-mindedness—and how could you possibly hope to share; or do any good at all by attempting to imagine? And again—how long before I might have been chatting cheerfully to some friend on the telephone or selecting with Brad the DVD we thought we'd like to watch?

"Or what about this, boy? 'He came to know he lacked compassion.' That's at least some slight improvement ain't it?"

"'But came to know a bit too late. He was such a dunderhead.'"

"Seems to me this inscription is getting longer and longer." The sheriff chuckled. "Poor stonecutter will sure need to put in some danged overtime. Seeing as how there are other things could just as easily be added."

"'In fact to tell the truth he probably always knew. Just never did anything about it.' I feel it in my bones: this stonecutter isn't going to care for me a lot."

"Unless he's getting paid by the word—and twice as much for the long uns."

We laughed; although in truth there wasn't much to laugh about.

"Them weren't the other things I was thinking of anyways."

He lifted his boots down from the corner of the desk. Took up his bunch of keys and walked unsteadily towards the door of my cell. "Hell's bells a man gets awful stiff," he said.

"Why are you letting me out? Even if I'm more or less right about what I've been charged with I don't see how I can make up for it. *Is* there any way I can make up for it?"

"Never say die boy," he answered. "Never say die." Again he took the straw from his mouth. He contemplated it like there was writing there: very small print that he couldn't quite decipher. "But . . . what's done is done. Don't you go leaning over backwards to think that you're a bad person."

"Thanks." I was now standing on the outside of the cell and shook his hand. "But it's a fairly new experience," I continued drily. "Perhaps you oughtn't to discourage it."

(In fact—to be entirely accurate—it wasn't all *that* new an experience, not by any means.)

Yet in any case he ignored it.

"Because if it was up to me," he said, "which it's not; but if it was . . . I'd do my best to see you didn't swing. And that's the truth of it boy."

I gave him a hug.

12

DOUBLE FEATURE?

Or work experience? It *felt* more like work experience. Much! There seemed no way on earth that I could simply have been sitting on my butt. There seemed no way on earth that I couldn't have been actively involved.

I don't mean in a film. I mean for real.

Right there outside the window the old woman was giving the old man a blow job.

"Oh come on Gertie do you *need* to make it quite so public? We'll have the police back here again."

I expostulated further.

"Besides. Who ever knows where that thing's been?"

The woman didn't so much as pause. Her lank grey matted hair fell forward from her grubby neck and it looked—though mercifully didn't smell—like someone had been sick down the back of her dress. Six inches to the right of where she knelt there was a newish pile of dog's muck.

The man, however, sitting with his ragged-trousered legs stretched out across the gateless cement forecourt and with his brown-jacketed shoulders resting against the windowsill (it didn't strike me as too comfortable) did in fact cast me a look. A drunken distracted conspiratorial look. He winked at me too as though to say, "You after me mate. If you're smart and play your cards right." Then his eyes lost focus and he gave himself up once more to his enjoyment.

I couldn't just use force and pull her off him.

"Well I'll go and fetch the garden hose, set that on the pair of you!" We all knew it was an empty threat. I think I even delivered it like the punchline to some joke.

"Yes you do that lad," said the old man. "You just do that."

But the sad thing was—he wasn't an old man. Well one of the sad things. It shocked you each time that you remembered. He was forty-eight; looked every bit of sixty-eight. Gertie was indeed in her sixties, late sixties, could easily have been his mother although she was no more connected to George than she was to any other bloke who ever used the refuge; she was just fairly free with her favours. George had been a teacher who'd had a fling with one of his fourteen-year-old pupils. His wife had left him. He'd never seen any of his three daughters again. He told us he'd once lived in a six-bedroomed house, detached, in the nicest suburb of Birmingham, a house that had cost about a hundred and fifty grand. Now he sat on the cement and let a woman who was twenty years older than him (when he had ruined his life for a girl at least twenty years younger) join him in a highly public performance of indignity and sleaze.

We knew hardly anything about Gertie's history. Gertie herself knew hardly anything about Gertie's history.

I went back inside. "Well you have to make the gesture," remarked my colleague Bill—we called him Beanpole—who was in the kitchen beginning to prepare the evening meal. "Admittedly a bit token but now at least we can try to pretend we haven't seen."

This was made a little difficult by the cries of another inmate who was standing at the window in the recreation room. Earlier I'd closed the window and pulled across the curtains but this bloke had drawn one of them back and was bawling his encouragement through the glass. "Go on Gertie! Attagirl! Doin' a gran' job. Mus' be comin' up to juice time." When I strode over and—perennial spoilsport that I was—again pulled across the thin patterned curtain he stopped feeling himself up through the pocket of his trousers and said, "Got a cigarette yer fucker?"

"No Joey I don't smoke. You know I don't smoke."

"Forget them cigarettes. Just ask 'im about fags," advised a raucous voice from the further end of the ping-pong table. Alf and Ron were currently taking a breather.

I turned in some surprise. I hadn't thought there was anything about me that was camp.

"No offence," added Alf. "Takes all sorts. You're a good bloke really. One o' the best," he said to Ron who'd only come that afternoon.

All of which appeared to be a little beyond the present comprehension of old Joey. He *was* old: halfway through his eighties.

"Gimme a cigarette yer fucker."

When I told him again that I hadn't got any he swung round and took an ineffectual swipe at me. It could have been half-playful but he lost his balance and fell. Thereupon he gave a ripsnorting fart and shat his pants and amid the resulting cheers and hoots of easy laughter a pool of urine spread across the mottled flooring.

"Oh God." Joey was immensely fat. No way could I have raised him on my own. "Have you hurt yourself?"

And only that morning he had shown me with pride a snapshot taken in Blackpool immediately postwar. He had been lean and looked athletic. Handsome in a flash sort of way. You could guess he had a comb in his rear pocket; was always slicking back his Brylcreemed hair. A bosomy blonde in ankle-strapped high heels hung on possessively to his thickly muscled arm.

I called to Bill and another colleague supposedly on his break to help me lift him. There were two or three relatively young men in the room but though in their way amiable enough none appeared to have much idea of what was going on or what might be required of them. Besides. If anybody was about to strain his back all those poor sods already had far more than enough to contend with.

I said again, "Joey are you hurt?" And to my pair of workmates: "Should we telephone the doctor?"

"Yer should've given me a cigarette yer fucker. Look what yer'd'ave saved." It was even with the glimmer of a smile of triumph that he glanced from me to the other two. "Haven't any of yer got one bleedin' cigarette among the three of yer? Talk about a load of fuckers!"

"*He's* all right," said Alan. "Aren't you Joey? God but what a whiff! We'll get you to your feet and then we'll have to leave you in the capable hands of young Danny here who'll get you all spruced up for your supper."

"Thanks," I said. "Thank you so very much. Just the kind of treat I always dreamed of."

"One of the perks of the profession," called out Alf who was evidently keeping an eye on us. "You get to take Joey in the shower with you! You get to take Joey in the shower! No offence mind. We got to 'ave our little joke."

In fact my own earlier little joke hadn't been entirely without basis. Hosing people down was a prominent feature of our work in the refuge. Because a hands-on approach was definitely not advocated; rubber-gloved or not. The cutting away and disposal of fouled-up clothing was already sufficiently stomach-turning.

After Joey I got George. (Beth, lucky thing, won Gertie.) The only way that I could get George to co-operate was to give him an ultimatum: "No shower no sausages!" And the damned thing was I'd have had to keep to that and then later cook him a fry-up. But thankfully this wasn't called for: first I hosed down the guy who had once walked along the promenade with an independent air and then I got the one who'd apparently lived in a house in Solihull which might now be worth a cool half-million; and I could honestly have cried at the drooping fat of the first and the premature aging of the second and the fact that both of them had lost the plot. I had a reasonable idea of what had happened to George; yet what on earth had happened to Joey? I had at one time asked him about his experiences in the war but I might just as well have asked what he remembered of being inside his mother's womb. It struck me now that if this were too often the way of things—and who ever had the slightest idea of what might lie ahead?—I was indeed quite lucky to have snuffed it young.

Although in truth I still kept on forgetting that I *had* snuffed it young. Still kept on forgetting that I had snuffed it at all.

In the kitchen afterwards when it was little short of midnight Beth and Alan and I sat over a mug of hot chocolate. Beanpole had gone home; Alan himself should have knocked off nearly an hour ago. Beth said: "I think I've had about as much of all this as I can cope with. I've decided I'll be getting out soon. The moment they can find themselves some other idiot."

"Don't blame you," answered Alan. "Can't think what keeps any of us here longer than a single day."

"Idealism," said Beth. She was twenty-one; looked older. Round-faced, round-figured, with mousy hair already thinning. But in a way that would never have occurred to me before . . . me with my penchant for the instantly nice-looking . . . she herself was in fact nice-looking. It was easy to see how, almost without having to go to any effort, death would make her beautiful. "You really believe that you can change the world."

"But you can," I smiled, "you can! Just because you may be doing so only in exceedingly small ways doesn't mean it's any the less worthwhile."

They looked at me, both of them, with an air of surprise. "Well who'd have thought it?" remarked Beth at last. "Pollyanna is alive and well!"

Amazingly I didn't bridle at the comment like I knew I would have done when I was younger. "I only wish I could be worthy of her!" I gave a mighty yawn. "But I know of course it's so easy just to say these things about improving the world piecemeal . . . Talk comes very cheap."

"Though what you said was right. Oh I don't know. Maybe it's just because I'm tired right now. Not quite the best time for arriving at any important decision."

There was a pause.

"With me," said Alan, "it's a kind of penance. Used to think these people were the dregs of society. Never felt the least concern for any one of them."

My eyes had been practically closing but I jerked them open with a sensation of near-shock.

Were there two of us here then?

I studied him more closely. He was a few years older than me; just turned thirty. Sandy-haired, snub-nosed, freckled. Shortish; stocky. By disposition jaunty.

"And what do you think now?" asked Beth.

"What do I think now? Oh that I was absolutely right. They are quite undeniably of course the dregs of our society."

A moment went by. He laughed at our expressions.

"That was a joke you mutts. No. I feel that every day and in every way I'm becoming a little more saintly and understanding. With any luck at all—by the time I'm fifty—people will automatically throw up at the sight of me."

"Yet you'll no doubt get to heaven a lot faster than the rest of us," I said. "Well a lot faster than me anyhow. They'll probably think I need a crash course. A whole series of crash courses. Which could last practically for ever." (Indeed, a blurry image flashed across my mind—an old lady in a hospital corridor?—but I couldn't get a grip on it. Neither then nor later.)

"Don't be daft," he smiled.

But I knew from his lack of more significant reaction that he was just one of those good people who didn't keep procrastinating. Who'd got his priorities right. Who wouldn't need to go to jail.

And I suddenly wondered: is that what I'd been doing? Procrastinating? Had I banked on maybe having another fifty years before I needed to be made *too* uncomfortable by my priorities?

I would once have felt jealous of Alan. Intensely jealous. Been all scornful and disparaging.

I said: "I wish you'd shown your saintly qualities a little earlier then. *You* could have taken Joey into the shower."

But surprisingly in fact I found I didn't really wish that at all. Not in the slightest.

13

I HAD JUST BROKEN UP WITH JONATHAN. It was raining when I got off
the No 16. The rain suited my mood but even so I didn't want to get
too wet; I pretty much ran to the Quebec. Just as I got there this man
was coming out. Our eyes met, my pulse rate quickened and I half
thought about following him. But no—no way! To tell the truth he'd
seemed a little down at heel and even with somebody who looked as
he did I wasn't in the market for any one-night stand.

However, he'd clearly thought I looked interesting as well, because
he'd turned around and re-entered the bar. Within a minute we were
swapping names.

"I'm Brad Overton," he said.

"Danny Casement."

As we shook hands something intangible about the glance he
directed at my face prompted me to say, "We haven't met before have
we?" In a place like the Quebec although I'd only been there a hand-
ful of times previously such a thing was perfectly possible. Or it could
have been at some other gay bar. In Soho perhaps. "I know that sounds
a bit corny."

"No not at all. But if we had met I'm sure that I'd remember."

"Me too. Ridiculous I asked."

"What'll you have to drink?"

"Oh that's kind of you. I think . . . a Scotch."

He ordered two. In response to the barman's usual query he said, "Oh—Grant's, that's fine," then asked me if I wanted water. We went and sat on one of those crescent-shaped sofa-things and had it to ourselves—the pub wasn't busy. Shirley Bassey who was always something of a favourite with us gays was singing 'My Way'. Happily they'd got her toned down a bit.

I said, "Cheers! Thanks," and clinked my glass against his. "So if we've never before met, at least one of us doesn't come here all that often."

"This is only—I think—my third time."

"Snap!"

The phrase went through my mind *Third time lucky?* (because Jonathan himself had happened on the second occasion) but I impatiently dismissed it. His appearance wasn't exactly shabby but he didn't look as though he took much pride in it. His blue-checked shirt was crumpled; his hair gave the impression that he patronized the cheapest barber in town. Which was a shame because it was good hair. Equally—I liked what the open top button of that unironed shirt revealed.

"In fact," he told me, "I'm still quite new to the gay scene."

"Mm?"

"I was married for almost twenty years," he said. "My wife and I have only recently split up."

"Twenty years? It must have been a good marriage?"

"I think so. Hope so. And we have a daughter whom we both love."

"Was it—just tell me to shut up if I'm being too personal—was it the sex part that went wrong?"

"Not principally. Naturally I'd always known I was bisexual but done everything I could to suppress the gay side"—he shrugged— "until when the marriage was over it all came back with a startling whoosh and is now doing its very damnedest to make up for lost time."

He pulled a face and picked up his drink from the table in front of us.

"No it was far more a question of money. Hélène who'd always been incredibly supportive just got tired of being poor. Quite suddenly. 'You live on a diet of pure hope,' she screamed, 'and if I ever hear again *It's going to be all right we'll somehow muddle through* I think I shall go mad. End up either in Holloway or Broadmoor. Life sentence for homicide!'"

"Justifiable homicide," I smiled. "Oh I'm sorry, perhaps I shouldn't have said that. But I can see her point of view."

"So could everybody else." He again made a grimace mainly expressive of self-mockery. "For twenty years or more I'd had a succession of crap jobs—never a career—because the only career I was ever interested in proved to be frustratingly elusive."

We'd finished our drinks.

"Same again?" I asked.

"Yes. Same again," he said. There was something mildly weird about the emphasis he seemed to lay upon those words. I liked him but—well it was difficult to analyze—was it simply that he came across as needy? That he was confiding in me too fully and too fast? (Though I knew I'd been displaying interest.) Or possibly it wasn't so much the things he was telling me as just a feeling I had about him: due maybe to a certain intensity that showed in his expression—indeed in the whole of his body language. And was it this which had made me think of neediness? And which now told me to be wary?

Very probably.

Yet physically the man was undeniably attractive. Mega-attractive. Dress him more stylishly, take steps to rectify that haircut and he'd have the sort of looks that could have got him out to Hollywood. From what he'd told me he had to be at least forty; but in my own view men only really came into their own when they hit forty.

And there was something too about his face—I mean other than the fact that it was handsome. Something innately appealing; something that reached out to me. Trustworthy? Vulnerable? In some strange way it made me feel . . .

No! I did not *want* to feel protective! In no way did I want to feel protective! Rather, if already I was beginning to look for someone new (which to be frank yes I suppose I was), I'd be looking for somebody who was himself protective. That had been the trouble with Jonathan;

or anyway part of it. He was only twenty-nine. He'd been immature. Obviously. Had too many unresolved hang-ups. Which meant of course he hadn't had the time to devote himself to mine! That thought made me laugh a little while I stood there waiting at the bar.

I threw a glance across my shoulder at this new guy, Brad Overton; and discovered him staring at me. If it didn't sound too crazy I'd have said his expression was . . . imploring? The eye-to-eye contact lasted for perhaps five seconds; totally unsmiling. Then at last we did smile— briefly—before I turned again to face the bar.

This time we had doubles; I thought he could most likely do with one. Also I decided to switch from Grant's to Bell's. Bell's was only slightly more expensive and I didn't know if either of us would even notice the difference but at least it represented some sort of nod towards the good life. I was always making such futile little gestures. Living in a bedsit in Cricklewood—and working at Price-As-You-Like-It—you needed to keep on reminding yourself that it really did exist. The good life.

He commented on the quantity yet not the quality; commented gratefully. "Now tell me about this elusive career of yours. Although I bet I can tell you what it is. And if I'm right then we're both tarred with the same brush. Heaven help us."

"Yes—indeed. Heaven help us. But tell me what you think it is."

"You're an actor who's waiting for his big break."

"Warm. Are *you* an actor?"

"No I've been vaguely toying with the idea, that's all. But this isn't about me. The spotlight's full on you."

"Well. I hope to be a playwright. So far I've written eight plays. Producers have often made some nice noises but it's never got beyond that. Up till now."

Because he'd put stress on that last phrase I was able to pretend optimism. Even eagerness. "Things show signs of changing?"

"Yes but you'd have to ask Hélène about that. According to me things always did show signs of changing."

It struck me as very sad that even mock eagerness and mock optimism were so totally out of place. "Then how do you manage to live?"

"Right now? I pop along every fortnight to those nice people at the

Job Centre who very sweetly pay me for my autograph. Perhaps they think that one day I'll be famous."

"Oh right," I said. And studied to keep my tone neutral. Myself, I had never once signed on. I hadn't got much patience with anyone who did.

"But—who knows?—that could be coming to an end. Just this afternoon I sent off three copies of the new play which I'm convinced is going to be my masterpiece. In fact that's why I'm here tonight—to celebrate."

Despite everything I suddenly felt glad I'd bought us doubles.

"Three copies?"

"Three different managements," he smiled.

"No but I mean—there must be many more than that?"

"Oh indeed there are. In another couple of weeks I'll maybe send off several others. It's just that . . . well photocopying gets expensive."

"Oh. Yes. Right." I nodded noncommittally. "What's this new one called?"

"*A Hundred Years Hence*,"

"Why? Is it set in the future?"

"No quite the reverse: it's set in the nineteen-twenties. A comedy; practically a farce. But when I was young I grew fond of this old man who used to lodge with my grandmother. 'A hundred years hence!' he'd always say if life was getting him down in any fashion. Say it with a little chuckle. 'A hundred years hence Mr Bradley sir . . . and what will any of this matter?' I used to find it quite comforting."

"But couldn't it be quite depressing too?"

He laughed. "Well just so long as my play still matters! And maybe one or two other equally worthwhile things."

"I like a man with confidence."

Brad picked up his glass and without drinking simply cradled its coolness for a moment. "Yes I do have confidence!"

He said this as though it were something he'd only just discovered about himself. But apparently it wasn't.

"In fact I always was confident," he added. "That little cry was merely in the nature of a reaffirmation of faith."

"Good."

"Expressing both my certainty and my defiance," he continued.

"Still good," I smiled.

"But one gets weak. I mean when one finds oneself wanting any particular thing too much it's amazing how the very silliest of doubts can sometimes start to filter through . . . Like weevils getting into cornflakes."

His simile almost reminded me of something. Though I couldn't remember what.

"Isn't it the Buddhists," I asked, "who claim that's the one true path to happiness? Learning never to want anything too much?"

He looked at me. "I don't know," he replied, "I don't know." His answer was ambiguous and either way slightly surprised me.

"Anyhow," I said—and raised my glass. "Good luck to *A Hundred Years Hence!* Let's hope there are certainly a few things that'll really go on mattering." Like the way we're all conducting our lives at this very moment I thought—and at every other moment too. But I didn't give voice to that one; I hadn't the slightest inclination to bring in anything about religion.

We drank. "Thank you," he said. "That was kind. You're a kind person."

This made me feel impatient. "Not true. Unfortunately. You don't know the first thing about me."

"Is that so? Then you're not kind? But in that case what's your own definition of kindness?"

"I'll tell you what my definition *isn't*. Not just when the occasion warrants it, not just when you happen to be with your family or your friends and it's the social, convenient, reciprocal, *expected* way to behave."

"But that wasn't at all the sense in which I meant it," he said. "A deep fundamental niceness . . . an obvious and intrinsic goodness of heart. Impossible to hide under a bushel even when a person tries his best to do so. Those were the only things I had in mind."

This didn't sound like just the small talk of two strangers in a pub. Not to put too fine a point on it it sounded like the conversation of a weirdo. I'd have said that he was speaking with conviction and sincerity but since there was clearly no basis for his doing so I found it all a tad alarming—possibly more than just a tad. I did what I could to change the subject: in fact the absolutely obvious thing.

"Are you ready for another drink?"

"No it's my turn."

I shook my head. "You can send me a ticket to your new play when it's the hottest thing in the West End."

"I'd like to think I shouldn't need to send it. That by then I might be seeing something of you. Or am I being a bit too forward?"

I paused. "Listen. I'm going to be frank with you. I think you're enormously attractive but . . ."

He waited. Well clearly I couldn't say It isn't any part of my plan ever to get involved with losers; not even with losers who look the way you do. I *would* contemplate a one-night stand—or even a six-night stand—could find myself thoroughly tempted to break a well-established rule; which in itself ought to make you feel quite privileged and proud. But I know that if I did, your wretched neediness could make the eventual separation painful to us both. And separation would be inevitable. The thing is, you see, I'm a materialist; and no power in heaven or on earth is ever going to change that. I can't afford to let myself get even passingly attached to a no-hoper. Oh passingly maybe—but who could say how long that 'passingly' would last or how much it might turn out to affect us?

My thoughts were getting repetitious. I was distractingly aware of some singer on the tape—I had no idea who she was—who had taken over from Abba, who had taken over from Liza Minnelli, who had taken over from Shirley Bassey; and I listened for a moment, perhaps only to give myself more time to compose the rest of my reply: ". . . And shall I recognize/the light in his eyes/which no other eyes reveal/or shall I pass him by/and never realize/that he was my . . . ideal?"

My silence must have stretched a full fifteen seconds; maybe longer.

"But . . . ?" he repeated at last, almost matching the sadness of the song with the sadness of that single syllable.

"But I've just broken up with my current boyfriend," I said, "literally just a couple of hours ago and I don't feel I'm yet in a proper frame of mind to . . . to start talking about seeing anybody else. I'm sorry."

I looked pointedly at my watch. I'd totally forgotten I'd just offered to get him another drink. "I think in fact I ought to be leaving." I stood up and extended my hand.

"No," he said. "Please don't go. Not just yet. Please." He smiled in some embarrassment. "I know that's totally the wrong thing to say."

Well at least it was something he should realize it. And in all fairness I had to concede that from his own viewpoint there wasn't any longer any right thing to have said. But although it was flattering to have become an object of such interest to a personable stranger and my instinct told me there was not the least degree of danger in him it wasn't—well if I can say this without sounding too abysmally blasé or conceited or spoilt or whatever—it wasn't by any means a new experience. One had to be a little hard.

"You could give me your phone number," I suggested. "Then maybe when I've got myself sorted out . . ." That 'maybe'; I was very careful to make sure it was included.

"No," he replied. "Once you walk out of here alone, I know damned well I've lost you. Lost you for all time," he added.

God!

God! God! God!

"Brad," I said. "Please! Less than an hour ago we hadn't even met." I hadn't intended to advance any more argument than that. I'd intended merely to say goodbye. But there was something about his eyes, some look in his eyes I couldn't simply turn my back on. The creature was suffering; I had unwittingly been the cause of it; and no matter how neurotic or disproportionate his pain . . . Besides. For some reason I really felt a liking for him. A deep liking. Perhaps I was nearly as unhinged as he was, we poor couple of sods.

"I know I'm doing this all wrong," he repeated. "But that isn't your fault. Please. They've got to make allowances. Stay just a little longer."

Honestly! His 'please'; my 'please'. The air seemed fraught with the echoes of our pleas.

"What do you mean they've got to make allowances? And who are they?"

He silently shook his head and in the face of his unhappiness my questions appeared a bit beside the point. He probably meant the

Fates; Frank Sinatra had spoken about those at some length in a film called *Young at Heart*.

"Yes you are doing it all wrong," I told him gently. I resumed my seat and took his hand and began to stroke it almost automatically; feeling rather like a father who was having to explain things, perhaps the very facts of life, to his touchingly ignorant young son. "Brad I realize that you're wholly new to this game and are really wanting—like you said—to make up fast for what you think's been lost. But you need to lighten up old thing; you truly do. Otherwise it seems to me you could easily be in line for a breakdown. Which anyway after all the stresses of separating from a wife you're clearly fond of wouldn't come as the most surprising thing on earth . . . surely? Not to mention endless years of money worries, talents unrecognized and a total lack of job satisfaction. It can't even be a lot of fun having to sign on at the Job Centre." Incredibly I found I had to resist a strong inclination to put my arms about him. "But Brad," I said. "*But . . . !*"

But Danny too. Why on earth had I been going down that particular road? A road which very plainly proceeded nowhere? I got back—fast—to the essentials.

"But I just can't emphasize it enough. You must *not* come on so strong. That way you'll only scare people. I promise. Whereas if you'd simply learn to relax you'd have no end of success. Probably more than you could manage. You're far and away the best-looking man in here tonight"—I glanced about us and attempted to give him a heartening smile—"which I admit isn't saying an awful lot but let me put it another way: I think you're one of the best-looking men I've ever met and I fancy you like mad and if I walked out of here with you tonight and we ended up in bed we'd probably have a really great time and—" I had to break off abruptly. "Yet I know it would only end in trouble and in heartache; possibly more for me than for you; so you can see that in a way I'm just being very selfish . . ."

And patronizing I thought. Oh hell. But still. To give comfort was my overall priority. Forget about everything else.

"Just look," I added. "All around us there are people giving you the eye, only waiting for me to get the heck out of here before they commit every foul beneath the sun to be the first to hijack my position."

He didn't give so much as a glance at all those supposedly wild-eyed ruthless competitors straining at their starting blocks.

"Why possibly more for you than for me?" he asked.

"What?"

"Heartache?"

"Oh. Because I'm not after casual sex. I'm after a relationship."

"Which only means you're not after a relationship with me?"

"No. Because you're not yet ready. First you've got to sleep around. Got to get rid of that whole crazy whoosh-factor thing. It'll take at least a year; possibly three. And believe me. You just won't want to be tied to anyone and needing to tell lies while all of that is going on."

Positively parental still. For the moment it wasn't a bad feeling. Like a father I really hoped my advice was going to be truly the best advice. Like a father I keenly, almost desperately, wanted to help. All in all I might have made a fairly good dad.

"I promise you—I promise you Danny—as God is my witness I promise you—I have no desire whatever just to sleep around. You couldn't want the right man any more than I do. And in you I know I've found the absolutely right man. Don't ask me how I know. I couldn't even begin to tell you but ours would turn out to be one of the happiest of partnerships on record. The almost perfect love affair—I *know* it."

"Don't," I said warningly. "Stop it. Can't you hear yourself? You're starting to do it again."

But anyway I went on stroking his hand to show that this time I wasn't going to let it scare me.

"And while you're about it you've got to rid yourself of one thumping great illusion. You can't go around believing in the almost perfect love affair. Not in this world. You're a fully fledged adult. You're talking like some foolish and romantic kid of twenty-four."

"Is that your age? Twenty-four?" But he spoke as if the question was wholly immaterial; anything—so long as the conversation just shouldn't be allowed to lapse.

I nodded. "Can't you tell? All those stars in my eyes? Not like that old cynic I'll become by the time I get to be . . . around forty?"

"Forty-three. Is that too old for you?"

"No."

"What then?"

"Oh God Brad!" I dropped his hand. I hardly knew the guy. "It isn't that you're too old for me. You're just too poor for me. There! Will that do? You'd never have stood the slightest chance—because you've latched on to a shameless little gold-digger! So you needn't worry that you've played this game all wrong; you couldn't possibly have played it right. On the other hand, old friend, you could have been as needy as all get-out, you could have come on just as strong as ever you felt like, if only at the same time you'd had the foresight to be rich!"

This speech was to some degree calculated. It was true but it was calculated. At least it should mean that instead of regretting me—the face in the street which you remember all your life—he might see me go with something like relief, rejoicing at the narrowness of his escape.

I italicized the point, upper-cased it. "You see I'm not at all a kind person. I'm a bastard. Totally self-centred, totally money-orientated, totally on the lookout for some poor old unsuspecting meal ticket. It doesn't sound as though your wife Hélène ever used to nag you. If we'd somehow come together—through sex—and somehow stayed together for a year or two—through sex—I know that me, I'd have become a complete shrew. I'd have nagged you incessantly; made your life pure hell."

"I don't believe that," he said. He was looking shocked. He was actually looking a bit white.

"Well there was maybe a *touch* of exaggeration. I'm not sure I'd have nagged you *incessantly*. I might have needed to get some sleep on occasion."

But he didn't respond in kind if that's what I'd been hoping. I really couldn't see why he appeared so utterly forlorn: merely an hour's encounter. And it wasn't as though I'd said he was too short—or too fat—or had halitosis. I hadn't even criticized his haircut. Nor was he to know that I considered his being poor as blameworthy; it was almost a requisite for an aspiring persevering undiscovered writer to suffer for his art—I hadn't said it but that was the impression which I'd aimed to give: the ennoblement conferred by starving in a garret. I thought that in a way I'd actually been tactful. And yet . . . he now looked desolate.

"There! Doesn't that make you feel any better? None of it your fault. *You couldn't have changed a bloody thing.*" I picked up his hand again; gave it a quick squeeze. "I think I ought to go."

But oddly I myself now felt quite drained; couldn't make the effort to get up. "We're a right pair," I said. "When we came in, perhaps the healthiest-looking couple in the room. But look at us now."

He appeared to pull himself together a bit. "You need that other drink," he said. "We both do." He stood up.

"No. You can't afford it. I was going to get it anyway—don't you remember?—before I forgot." We both laughed, a little shakily. I too stood up. He pushed me back down.

"But while I'm gone I trust you not to make your getaway."

"I won't."

Three minutes later he returned with two more double whiskies. "You'll notice I didn't even glance? You'll notice how much confidence I had that you were going to keep your word?"

"Yes at least I can say I always keep my word. But I wish you'd let me pay for these. You ought to bear in mind that photocopying."

"Why would you want to pay for them when obviously there's no way you're going to benefit from it?"

"Oh the exception that proves the rule? And I wouldn't want to leave you thinking as how I'm *all* bad."

"Why not?"

"Because although you might never guess it I quite like you. In fact I like you quite a lot."

"Why? When plainly I'm a loser?"

"Dunno," I said. "And it isn't just the way you look. There's something about your personality. I feel that in happier circumstances—i.e. if you were loaded—we could easily have made a go of it."

"Me too."

"You see then: there's a lot we have in common. And incidentally. I never said you were a loser."

"You didn't have to. Tell me something though. May I be serious again for one minute?"

"Oh God must you?"

I smiled—decided not to mention that if there'd been any marked letup in seriousness then obviously I'd missed it.

"Are you proud of being the way you are?" he asked. "Regarding your attitude to money?"

"No of course not. I'm faintly proud of *recognizing* I'm the way I am. But that's all."

"Meaning that to be aware of some fault is already half the battle?"

"Not really." I shrugged then shook my head. Apologetically. "I'm not entering any battle."

Disbelief. Disbelief and further deflation. "You're telling me you wouldn't want to change?"

"Would I want to change?" Clearly it wasn't bad he should feel yet more disillusioned in me but all the same . . . "Yes I suppose I would. In a better world. But in this present one it seems to me a completely valid approach. Hold out for all the pleasure you can get. You need to be happy; if in the end you haven't had plenty of sheer enjoyment you must accept the fact you've been a failure. And just so long as you're always careful not to harm anybody . . ."

"Except yourself. What happens when finally you've got to answer for your own love of money? The love of money that's the root of all evil?"

"Oh come off it Brad. If your talking about judgment—and your quoting from the Bible makes me think that you're a Christian—then shake hands: me as well: I'm a Christian too." (I almost set those last four words to music; my mother had once been in an amateur production of *Annie Get Your Gun*.) "And because of that or in spite of that I think it's practically my duty to make the most of every minute in every way I can. Which inevitably takes money."

"But if you're a Christian you have to remember what Jesus himself said on the subject of riches."

"Yes well Jesus never had to live in a bedsit in Cricklewood. He'd never been to a motor show or leafed through *Homes and Gardens* or dreamed of owning a Harley-Davidson. I bet he'd never heard of Georgio Armani. He wasn't that keen on going to nightclubs or posh restaurants. Or to cinema or theatre."

He cut me short; dejectedly. "I think you've made your point."

"Not quite. Even in the Apocrypha it's never recorded that he went to San Francisco or Sydney or Portofino. He lived in the sunshine and life was simple and he was mainly among friends. And I'm the one supposed to nag, not you."

He ignored that last bit and went back to the sentence before it. "I wonder if he'd recognize how thoroughly easy he had it."

"At least in the evenings he didn't have to sit round and just twiddle his thumbs when there was nothing worth watching on the box and even going out to the pub was temporarily beyond him."

"Maybe he went visiting the lonely and the helpless? Made them a little less lonely and a little less helpless? I shouldn't have thought that required a vast financial outlay."

Two could play at that ignoring game. "Perhaps he was lucky: perhaps he didn't suffer from a low boredom threshold? For me, being bored with life is the ultimate sin but in order not to be bored with life you need to have dosh."

We stared at one another and I gave him a slow, provocative grin.

"I admit that right now I'm not exactly bored."

"People say the best things in life are free." He smiled. Thankfully parody was implied; not condescension. I wanted him to acknowledge that even my present state of non-boredom had cost us the price of several whiskies. I suppose I could have said it myself; I'd forgotten that he had paid for the last lot.

But I repeat: it was such a shame. (Not to mention such a cliché.) When he smiled I felt he could have won me over in just about any foolish argument on earth. (And if we *had* ever got together I would have regarded that as my very first duty: to make sure he smiled a lot—to introduce a regular dosage of leavening and frivolity.)

"Yeah," I said. "You're right. The best things in life are free. The flowers belong to everyone. So do the stars that shine. Let's add the public libraries and some few of the museums and art galleries. Well hallelujah! In fact a great many of the flowers *don't* but heaven forbid I'd ever choose to quibble. What, me?"

"Oh Danny," he said. The smile was entirely gone. He could have been about to cry.

I clearly had a nutcase on my hands. But one I thought I might have grown fond of—perhaps extremely fond of. Though again I'm doing nothing here but repeat myself.

I felt very glad he didn't cry.

"Don't be sad. You've got everything in life to look forward to. I take it you can't have forgotten *A Hundred Years Hence*, your very best work up until this present time: that masterpiece just waiting to be pounced upon?"

He shook his head, wretchedly. This wasn't to tell me that he hadn't forgotten it. This was simply to tell me that he'd given up hope.

"Oh Brad. Brad Brad Brad. What in heaven's name are we to do with you?"

He didn't answer. I stroked his hand again. It wasn't the right move. His eyes now definitely grew swimmy. (Quite stupidly mine did as well.)

"Hey!" I said. "What ever happened to all that confidence? That certainty; defiance? That grand reaffirmation of faith?"

He looked at me. He downed the rest of his drink. A tear slipped over one eye-rim but he brushed it away with abrupt resolution. "Come on. I want to buy you supper." He seemed a creature of seriously fast-changing moods.

"I've already had a sandwich."

"Tough! I'm going to buy you supper."

I swallowed the remainder of my own drink.

"You can't afford it," I told him. "For Christ's sake you've got to be single-minded: think photocopying! Photocopying! But I'll tell you what. I'll treat us both to a McDonald's. I'll come with you if you'll settle for that."

In fact I wasn't absolutely certain I had enough money but I thought oh well loaves and fishes—it *is* in a good cause. Or there again, if Jesus didn't seem totally convinced of this, then Brad himself might have to help out. But patently I hoped not.

"Okay," he said. "Thank you." He said it so simply and gratefully that I somehow felt impelled to take his hand and anyone watching us leave the pub—as indeed, I noticed, several people were—would have thought we were a couple, or at the very least heading for a night of rampant sex. I noticed it with a sensation that bordered on proprietorial pride.

But I hadn't been thinking. In the street I hastily released his hand.

The rain had stopped. We turned into Edgware Road. Neither of us said much; for the moment none too surprisingly we seemed to have talked ourselves out. But it felt companionable. We walked close without touching but again I very much wanted to touch—I should have liked for instance to place my arm around his shoulder or less obtrusively perhaps yet even more intimately slip my hand into his off-side back pocket. But this wouldn't have been at all fair since undoubtedly it would have raised his hopes; I'd already erred in that direction. Nevertheless I really had to discipline myself. And unexpectedly too I felt—well not precisely happy but—yes I shall always remember this evening I thought. I shall always remember this man.

We went on therefore, mute but companionable, for maybe something over five minutes. We came to a crossing called George Street. He turned to me and said, "Danny . . . ?" He somehow managed to inject into those two weak syllables (of which I'd never been immensely fond) so great a wealth of feeling that I might have imagined there was unalterable affection there, love and forgiveness and understanding, a huge undercurrent of need and an all-consuming plea; whatever he was about to say or ask or beseech could in no way have matched that initial astonishing intensity. He was obviously putting everything he had into the formulation of the sentence that would follow; was laying his very heart and soul on the line—his whole life (to continue in this current understated mode). It was the language of two people who were lovers and had got to know each other well; by no means the language of strangers who had just met. I could scarcely help but feel touched—a little paradoxically perhaps—and yet I was about to tell him, "Don't . . ." In fact I was about to tell him, "Don't . . . you don't have to do this," not even fully comprehending what I meant by that. But I didn't tell him. In his preoccupation he had stepped off the pavement and right into the path of a taxi.

14

THEY TOOK HIM TO ST MARY'S IN PADDINGTON and he was pretty badly hurt; at first they wondered if he'd even last the night. I said I was his partner—that way they let me sit beside his bed and keep a vigil over him and make a deal with God. Save him—*please*—and if you do . . . It was absurd, I still scarcely knew the man and yet suddenly I felt I knew him well and only wanted to be allowed to get to know him better. I should have seen him as unstable and yet instinct told me he was reliable and rocklike and the linchpin that I badly needed. I'd felt contemptuous of the twenty-year start he had on me and how little he had to show for it in hard material terms. Now? Fuck hard material terms I said to God. If he'd been rich he wouldn't have been needy; and he almost certainly wouldn't have been in that particular place at that particular time. It was quite a reversal but this same instinct told me that unless I was prepared to go with it I was definitely about to miss out. Instinct or sentimentality? Instinct or guilty conscience? I couldn't give a tinker's cuss. All I wanted was for Brad Overton to survive and be happy. No; I also wanted to apologize and to tell him it would be fun walking by his side into the future. More than fun I said to God; an absolute requirement. Come on I said insistently towards the dawn. Please save him. Please. I realize it's for my own sake more than his but I promise I'll never ask for anything again—I mean never anything again that's just for me. Or very largely for me. And I'll try to make up for past sins; it won't be easy but I'll really do my very best. By then I hardly knew what I was saying and when Brad eventually opened his eyes sometime after six I felt as if for every actual minute since last night's encounter I had somehow lived through an entire day. In the best tradition of old Hollywood movies I was holding his hand at that important moment and he was practically at once in a state of full consciousness. I told him I loved him. It didn't feel at all premature or strange. On the contrary. It felt exactly right.

You should have seen his face.

You would have said he looked an altogether different man to the one I'd sat with earlier. You wouldn't have known *quite* what made you say it but you'd have held onto your opinion.

I stayed with him another hour or so. Then I half-walked, half-ran—in a spirited resurgence of the rain—all the way back to Cricklewood. After a brief stop-off for some dry clothes I was about fifteen minutes late arriving at the shop; but when I made it my excuse that I'd just met the man who was going to change my life—after he'd got himself a decent haircut of course—the manager put her head on one side and gazed at me consideringly. Then she laughed and said that okay—in her own view anyhow—this was probably worth being a little late for. But why was it only that he was going to change my life? Why wasn't I going to change his?

15

THE DAY OF OUR FUNERALS HAD COME; it was time for me to leave the Halfway House. Both Isabella and Hermione kissed me *au revoir* and Richard saw me off at the front door.

"Listen," he said. "You'll be arriving far too early for the wake."

He was speaking quite casually but I knew there was nothing at all accidental about what he was telling me, nor about the fact that the four of us had eaten lunch an hour ahead of time.

"You know that primary school just round the corner?" He meant just round the corner from our home. "Since you'll have an hour or so to spare why not drop in?"

He gave me a parting hug and I have to say—although perhaps I ought to be ashamed to—that being hugged by Richard successfully allayed the fears I'd more than once experienced: that my sexual orientation had been in any way tampered with or, practically as bad, had now become irrelevant.

Possibly because of this I descended Pack Hill whistling: the tune Hermione had been humming before lunch. It was driving me crazy though, because I couldn't quite place it. Not until just before I reached the school. At which point it would probably have stopped niggling at me anyway: Richard hadn't mentioned a single thing about a teaching practice.

Teaching practice?

Teaching practice!

As though faced with a whole classroom of kids I'd have even the faintest idea of where to begin!

"Well we thought you might begin Mr Casement by telling us all a little about the Seven Deadly Sins." Miss Avery was a small cheerful-looking black woman in a bright yellow dress. She was about fifty. "Yes I think we'd all be interested to hear about those wouldn't we class? It's very kind of Mr Casement to spare the time to come and talk to us." She smiled at me and went and took a seat by the door. There was a prolonged scraping of chairs as the boys and girls, some twenty of them, mainly white and all about seven, now followed her example and busily sat themselves down.

"Quietly," she said reproachfully from the back. "Quietly now."

I stared briefly at the blackboard hoping for inspiration. She had already written down the title.

One of the boys put up his hand. "Please Miss—I mean sir—" there were giggles—"what *are* the Seven Deadly Sins?"

Impatient little beast; clearly couldn't wait! The pity was—he'd have to. Until someone came along who could actually tell him.

I mean I'd heard of them of course but hadn't got much notion of what in fact they were. Murder, rape, suicide, dictatorship? Dictatorship didn't sound precisely the kind of word you'd come across in the Bible, any more than terrorism did, either of the political or inner-city housing-estate variety; and how the heck was I going to explain rape? This wasn't fair I thought rebelliously. Even when someone was meant to be undergoing a test of some sort he should've been given a *small* amount of preparation. Surely?

"And what are sins?" asked another of my pupils, this time a girl.

Thank heaven for little girls as my sisters had once gone through a phase of telling me. I said: "Sins are the bad things we do which we all try not to. But which somehow we all carry on doing even when we're old and should by then know better."

"Why? Are they fun?"

"Yes. On the whole. I suppose." I sought for an example. "Like . . . like if we're rude to people. To our parents perhaps or to people in shops . . ." But no it hadn't been fun being rude to my parents—except in a cheeky humorous sort of way; otherwise it had simply been the result of bad temper. And as for people in shops— why should I have been rude to people in shops? I felt as if I'd backed myself into a dead end from which there wasn't going to be any chance of escape. "Or rude to teachers," I added desperately—maybe hoping to ingratiate myself. But I remembered all too clearly playing up some of the more ineffectual teachers at my own school. One in particular. ("Casement why haven't you handed in your homework?" "Yes sir I'm very glad you happened to bring that up; I was quite hoping to have a word with you about that, actually." The sort of craftily refined insubordination that won shamelessly easy acclaim from my classmates.) I supposed it had been fun; I'd obviously enjoyed the laughter—and the popularity; naturally I hadn't known that Mr Tibbotson was going to have a nervous breakdown. Hadn't known that he was going to put his head inside a gas oven. Christ! Why had I had to think about that? I once again hurriedly changed my example; hoped no one would realize it hadn't provided me with any good place to go. "Or like if we steal money out of our mums' purses," I said. "We think it's going to lead to fun."

"That's why we don't stop doing them even when we're old." We might have sort of covered that point already but really here was one bright class. At this rate these children might soon tell *me* the nature and composition of the Seven Deadly Sins.

"Why do we even try to stop doing them?" asked two others at virtually the same instant.

"Because I think that deep down we'd all like to be good. Like Jesus wanted us to be." I glanced at two Asian girls. "And Buddha and Mohammed too . . ." I floundered; I'd never taken a keen interest in comparative religion. "But of course it's harder to be good than to be selfish and mean and concerned only with the things that'll make *us* happy sod everybody else . . . Oh excuse me, I'm sorry, not a polite thing to say."

"My mummy sometimes says sod it."

"My daddy says fuck."

I held up both arms. "Hey—hey—hey!" But at least at this point if at no other so far every child was looking interested. I didn't dare glance even for a second towards the door.

"Sir? Are you good sir?"

"No I'm afraid not. I'd be a very poor example."

"But do you want to be?"

"Yes I'd like to have been, more than anything." I faintly surprised myself since it struck me I hadn't just said that because it was the sort of thing one ought to say.

Then I thought: More than anything? More for instance than having been allowed to get to the Quebec at the very moment when Brad was coming out? ("Oh hell. It's raining anyhow. There's just got to be time for another drink.") So in fact it wasn't even true was it? Just one of those things that was remarkably easy to say, and even felt sincere, but—

Brad I wonder what you were like at school. I really can't imagine you'd ever have behaved as I did. To Tibbotson I mean, old Tibbotson. (Youngish Tibbotson—still in his thirties?) I wish I'd known you when you were at school. No. When *I* was at school. Just think what a restraining influence you might have been.

But I'd forgotten. School. It made nonsense of the notion I'd sometimes had, that because I was raised to be considerate, I had always been considerate.

"And sir what does deadly mean?"

"Well . . ." I pondered. "In this case not so much something that will cause death as something that is very very serious." Oh help I thought. Apart from the meaning of seven there was nothing else left to ask. Well here we go then.

"Would it be a good idea if Mr Casement were to write down all the Deadly Sins?"

I had practically forgotten the presence of the headmistress.

No! Thank you Miss Avery. Not at all a good idea.

"Yes Miss," agreed the whole class instantly in unison. That bunch of little creeps.

Albeit that likable bunch of little creeps.

"He could just say a few words about each of them and then it will be time for break. I think that would be best Mr Casement; children like to see things written down." Bless their tiny hearts. She smiled at me encouragingly but the only bit of true encouragement had been contained in just three words. *Time for break.* Perhaps by the skin of my soul—and with the further aid of a no doubt quizzical but well-intentioned providence—I might manage to hold on.

I took up the stick of chalk, stood before the blackboard and considered.

Then plunged in.

Murder. Rape. Suicide. Oppression. Terrorism. Dishonesty. Hooliganism. Theft.

Not bad.

Not bad.

And let's face it these kids were never going to know. I could write down anything: spitting, blowing your nose without using a handkerchief, sticking your chewing gum beneath the seat. Filing your nails in public. And Miss Avery—I relied on it—wouldn't think of correcting me. Not in front of that sweet receptive audience. For the moment I was safe.

"Please sir that's eight!"

So it was. Well anyway a fault on the right side. I immediately looked about me for the duster; decided that perhaps I didn't need it.

"In Biblical times hooliganism wasn't always such a problem." Why wasn't it? "Football hooliganism that is. Nor was vandalism: you didn't get vandals ripping up train carriages or peeing in telephone boxes or standing on motorway bridges and dropping off lumps of concrete. Obviously we've got to keep up to date and modify a little whenever it becomes necessary. *Strictly* necessary," I added in an attempt to show I didn't take such alterations lightly. "In fact since the *seven* were first handed down to us," (Moses? Jesus? St Paul?) "we've been allowed to turn it into *eight* or even *nine*. Given a special dispensation, that's known as."

So for good measure I now added drunkenness to my list along with drug taking—changed that to pushing—though with a nod towards economy I did at least bracket them together. "In view of modern pressures and present-day social conditions . . . like for instance high unemployment," I told them vaguely, being extra careful, now that the seven had turned into the nine—with subdivisions—not to risk even the most fleeting of sideways glances in the direction of Miss Avery. I decided not to ask how many of their own dads were currently out of work but it seemed to me at least as relevant to try to warn them off becoming drug addicts as it did to try to warn them off becoming dictators.

However I also decided to do a little tidying up: crossed out rape, oppression and terrorism—substituted 'lust for power'. That reduced us by two; brought us back indeed to the recommended level. But I had already told them there were at least eight and they were clearly pretty hot at their arithmetic; I didn't want them beginning to think I had but a shaky grasp on my subject. I wrote down 'dishonour'; lengthened it into 'dishonourableness'; hoped to heaven it was a proper word.

("And if it wasn't before I don't know how the world ever got on without it!")

I pronounced it for them. "It means you can't be trusted. It means you say you'll do things . . . but then you just don't. It also means . . ." I hesitated. "Listen. Shall I tell you about a time when I myself was dishonourable?" I hadn't realized I was going to say this but I'd thought I heard Miss Avery stir and suddenly the words were practically dictating themselves. "When you're a bit older," I began, "you'll all start having boyfriends and girlfriends."

There was a lot more giggling and a lot of vehemently indignant denials. "Children! Children!" said Miss Avery.

She didn't say, "Teacher! *Teacher?*"

I smiled. "I once had a girlfriend." Dishonesty—even whilst expatiating on dishonourableness? "And she gave me a really nice present: two tickets for *Beauty and the Beast.*"

Forget about homicide, kidnapping, blackmail, hijacking—forget about every form of rape and pillage—*Beauty and the Beast* was what really got them. I had to explain it was the show and not the movie I was talking about. There raged a heated controversy over which of them had seen the film the greatest number of times. Miss Avery again needed to step in but even she couldn't prevent several muted yet impassioned attempts at getting the final word. Twenty times! Thirty! Seventy! Two thousand! I also had to explain that the tickets had been for row F in the stalls and had cost thirty-five pounds *each*. Maybe this was the only thing which could effectively have silenced them.

"Sir! Was she rich—your girlfriend?"

"One of the Spice Girls?"

"Victoria Beckham?"

"The Queen?"

I told them this had all happened at the start of the show's run and that the tickets had needed to be booked about six months in advance.

"In the meantime we split up: Philippa and I."

"Did you like it sir?"

"What, *Beauty and the Beast*? I thought it terrific. Magical. Enchanting. The best stage show I'd ever seen."

There was a chorus of approval: I was an all-right sort of guy. They had cut straight to the very heart of it; weren't nearly so interested in all those boring old preliminaries.

Or maybe just a few were.

"What did your girlfriend say?" . . . "Did you have another girl-friend by then?"

"Well that was the point. That's why I'm telling you this. When Philippa gave me the tickets it *was* a present of course but they were given on the unspoken understanding the two of us would see the show together; and really I was only looking after them because his work often took him abroad . . . *her* work often took *her* abroad I mean and without a lot of notice so that it was just possible I might have to find somebody else to go with . . ." I now felt slightly flustered and began to wonder why I'd started.

"And you did!" piped up one of them who was very plainly on the ball and looked as though he too might someday leave a trail of broken hearts.

Well in my own case hardly a trail. Merely the one. Philip's.

"At the time we broke up you see I'd forgotten all about the tickets. But then even after I'd remembered I just sort of hung onto them . . ."

I had addressed this last remark to the future potential heart-breaker—wondering to which sex those hearts would predominantly belong—and he, rather gratifyingly, repaid such individual attention.

"I bet you felt bad when you went to see it!"

"I should have done. And I do now. But you're completely right— you're all of you completely right—it was a highly dishonourable thing which I did and now I can't tell you how much I wish I hadn't." I pulled a face and spread my hands.

"Seventy pounds!" said one of the little girls. I told you Brad they were spot on with their mathematics.

But of course you never knew anything about this whole sad shabby episode did you? I always pretended to myself that it was trivial yet I suppose that long before this afternoon I must have felt thoroughly ashamed of it. (Though would I have felt any less ashamed if Jonathan had proved to be lastingly worth it? I hope not.) Why had it never occurred to me to try to make up for it in some way? Perhaps send Philip two top-price tickets for *The Lion King*?

If you *had* known, Brad, you might have suggested that; even have tried to pay for the tickets yourself you old softie. Neatly defeating the whole object of the exercise it hardly needs to be said. (Just as you nearly did in a very different context when trying to pay—at the same time as your yearly subscription—my own membership fee to Amnesty International. When wisdom sometimes failed you it was only because of well-nigh irrepressible generosity.)

"But you told us *Beauty and the Beast* was wonderful. What I don't see sir is how you could enjoy yourself so much. Not when . . . I mean not when you'd been . . . all dishonourable like that."

This frank yet somehow uncensorious observation came from my little heartbreaker; who one day Brad is patently going to be in your own world-beating class and simply romp ahead towards judgment. (Like Alan too, Alan at the refuge? But here I began to feel confused again and speedily returned my concentration to the present.) I only hope he's going to find his equal.

I only wish you had.

"I believe you may be much nicer than me," I told him. "But any-how. One slightly comforting thing. One of the messages of *Beauty and the Beast* is all about admitting you've been wrong and then finding out you've been forgiven. I certainly admit that I've been wrong and hope that I shall be forgiven."

"If I was Philippa," said one of the Asian girls very shyly, "I know I'd forgive you. And after that I'd like to marry you!" She swiftly brought her face down to the desk and buried her whole head beneath her arms.

There was uproar. Miss Avery came hurrying forward and stepped up onto the rostrum. I told the little Asian girl that I felt very grateful and very honoured but she persisted in keeping her face concealed from everybody's view. Her body proclaimed her to be giggling.

"Well class I'm sure we found that talk most interesting. Didn't we? I hope you're all going to say a big thank-you to Mr Casement for shedding such light on the subject of the Seven"—she paused and smiled at me and the smile turned into a chuckle—"of the Seven Eight or Nine, that is, Very Serious Sins." There was a renewed scraping of chairs and shuffling of feet; the children again stood up and during the ensuing stillness obediently responded, though in an almost risibly drawn-out fashion:

"Thank you Mr Casement."

"Perhaps Mr Casement will come back sometime to tell us about the Eleven or Twelve Commandments."

I hoped she wasn't muddling them; but reckoned she would probably return to sort the whole thing out immediately after the break.

"I think on the whole," I said shaking Miss Avery's hand, "it might be rather better if I didn't."

"Oh I don't know," she answered cheerfully. "I feel it all depends on whether you believe more in the spirit or the letter."

Conveniently Heartbreaker and my self-offered bride—who was now peeping sparkling-eyed through her fingers—were standing at adjoining desks. As I went out I gave a general smile and a wave but was able to smile at those two in particular. Which pleased me.

16

HOME!

The front door's open.

Conversation, laughter, teacups. And probably more people than at any two parties we had ever given.

Our funeral reception. Yours and mine Brad yours and mine. In that case is it possible, could it just be possible . . . ? In the doorway to the sitting-room I stand on tiptoe and crane my neck—as though without doing that we wouldn't have been tall enough, not you nor I, either to see or be seen. People appear to come and go right through me; at first it's disconcerting, soon I scarcely notice. From sitting room to dining room. To kitchen. Then into garden. Still more people with plates and teacups—amongst them one of my brothers talking to a mutual friend from school—I walk straight through them (no mainly I still go in between). Inside again, upstairs, into each of the three bedrooms, well two bedrooms and the one we'd made into your study; even push open the door to the bathroom. But by then of course I'm losing hope. You aren't here, you just aren't here. I suppose I hadn't really been expecting it—not after what Richard and Isabella had told me of your necessary departure from the inn—yet I'd been thinking there could conceivably be a big surprise awaiting me, you always liked to give surprises, been thinking that you'd charmed the others into becoming your collaborators. (A thought which had even helped me through that dismayingly muffed teaching practice.) Oh well. I tell myself it's stupid to feel so disappointed. I go back downstairs, now make a beeline for my mother. Naturally I love my dad as well but it's to my mum that I return for comfort.

She's speaking to the three old ladies—sisters—who'd been our closest neighbours, yours and mine; and I soon discover it's they who've made the sandwiches, cakes, scones and savoury tartlets. I don't know whether perhaps they've organized this whole reception but certainly they've always had a spare key to our cottage just as we had always had a spare key to theirs. Then I hear it's your parents who—although feeling too unwell to be able to get here this afternoon—have supplied the champagne (hey, champagne? *champagne?*) and hired the glasses. My own parents have provided the flowers—tremendous flowers as now I notice—which decorate the two main rooms.

But Brad. Even if your mum and dad haven't felt quite strong enough to face it several others in your family have. Two of your cousins have driven from Torquay; an uncle has come all the way from Scotland. So where are you my love . . . where in heaven's name are you? Surely you've got to be here somewhere? Invisible like me of course; invisible even *to* me? Then is it, for some reason, that we're just not allowed to see one another? Not allowed to communicate—not even through something as simple as a smile? But if that's the case it's cruel. That is so cruel. It makes me want to kick at something, slam my fist against the wall. Makes me want to say I've had enough of all this, what the bloody hell is going on? Eh God? What the bloody hell is going on?

(I seem to have forgotten that until I got here I wasn't absolutely *relying* on your presence. So am I just being inconsistent? Or does my anger arise more from standing in our home but knowing that 'home' has turned into a completely meaningless word now that I don't find you in it? Anger? Anguish, more like. I feel like a widow or a widower or anyone who's inconsolably bereft; and I seem really to experience, for the first time since Sunday morning—no, what do I mean?—for the first time ever, how it feels to be bereft.)

So, bemused, unhappy, I go and say hello to my father—symbolically. But hardly have I reached him than he breaks away from the small group he's been a part of and begins to round up everybody from the hall, dining room, kitchen and garden and shepherd them back to where he wants them. Meanwhile my two sisters are pouring the champagne and one of my brothers-in-law is circulating with a tray of it. Eventually, after the room has got so full that there's again a large overspill into the hall, my father, standing back against the fireplace in which there's now another magnificent arrangement in a borrowed vase, speaks slowly and clearly into that polite expectant hush.

"I know we've all been having a good time which I feel sure is exactly what Brad and Danny would have wanted—and I'm sorry if it looks as if I'm breaking up the party though I promise you I'm not—but perhaps the moment has arrived when we should all get together and share some thoughts or reminiscences about these two people whom we loved. And after that we'll all raise a glass and wish them *bon voyage*—in fact not simply a good journey but the very best it's possible for anyone ever to embark on. And let's hope and pray that in this they may have had a real headstart. Brutal though the time and manner of their setting out at least they did set out together. That in some hard way has to be a comfort not only to themselves but to the rest of us."

And my father begins to cry—my old dad actually begins to cry. He blows his nose and briefly wipes his eyes and I notice that by this time many others, both men and women, are similarly affected. Indeed (could you ever beat this for foolishness?) I myself am.

And yet, I think, we didn't set out together. Not quite; my dad is only trying to be tactful. And I mightn't be standing here now feeling anything like so desolate if we had.

But why am I feeling desolate? I think I really do believe you must be here as well, yes somewhere you must be here as well, at this very moment you could be standing right beside me . . . and yet . . . why can't I draw any solace out of such a thought, be given (once more) some reassuring sign? Logical conviction of closeness accompanied by total absence of communication seems almost like the very hardest thing. If only I could feel the faintest impression of a handclasp.

Logical? Well I suppose I can't be sure if it's *that* logical.

And something else: how true is it that in reality we were two people whom everybody here loved? Had my father himself, my father and mother themselves, actually loved you? No more I thought than your own parents had actually loved me. In both parental homes there had existed a conscious attempt at broadmindedness and goodwill but it wasn't just the fact of our being gay which had worried them, there was that big discrepancy in our ages. And I hadn't looked forward to our infrequent joint visits to your family any more than you'd looked forward to our infrequent joint visits to mine—we had unfailingly on every such occasion needed to gird our loins, it had become one of our silly little jokes, "Loins girded?"—and telephone inquiries from both sides as to the health of our respective partners had always seemed duty-driven and speedily disposed of. (I remember once saying to you, "When your mother asks 'And how is Danny?' you could easily say 'Dead' and she would answer, 'That's good and has anything of interest happened since we last spoke?'") And yet now, your parents, they must have had delivered I don't know how many cases of champagne; and—well despite these sentimental tears I've just had running down my cheeks and the genuine love or gratitude I'm feeling towards everybody gathered here I could still be tempted to call out, "But why didn't you love us quite so much whilst we were actually around?" I *could* call it out of course; I'm forgetting that nobody would hear.

My father's asking: "Is there anybody who'd like to add anything to that?" And immediately a host of hands go up. It reminds me of my experience a little earlier on. "Yes Sarah?"

Sarah's the younger of my sisters; only a year or two older than myself.

"I just want to say that I miss him . . . I miss Danny. He was as good a brother as you could possibly get. And Brad was like a really nice brother-in-law; someone we were truly glad to welcome into our family and someone whom we'd hoped to know better and better as the years went by."

Well that's all right: none of my siblings had shown themselves to have even the smallest difficulty about accepting you and whenever we had spent time with any of *them*, particularly in the absence of my parents, the atmosphere had been totally relaxed. Sometimes gay issues had been fleetingly discussed and sometimes amongst other jokes being told there'd been a gay one at which we'd all either laughed or groaned according to its quality; but mainly everyone's sexual preferences—although in such surroundings you and I had never felt too inhibited about showing each other our affection—had appeared to be taken wholly for granted, either forgotten about or regarded as irrelevant.

But.

He was as good a brother as you could possibly get. I tried to remember just one instance of my having deserved a plaudit such as that, as though even *one* instance would have rendered the statement fully valid, siphoned off all its extravagance. The most I could come up with was that I'd generally been cheerful and out of my five siblings had been the biggest clown, the one who'd oftenest made the others laugh: i.e. had possessed a natural ability to play the fool which had given *me* quite as much entertainment as anybody and at the same time had pandered to my vanity. But apart from that—what? Had I ever really put myself out? Ever mended anyone's puncture (unless I were getting paid for it) or taken over anyone's paper round (unless I were getting paid for it) or ever tried to entertain a brother or sister who was ill in bed (unless for some reason I too was feeling bored or had been begged by one or other of my parents please to do so)? And on the occasion that Simon had wrecked his own Lambretta had I then let him borrow mine although the speedy loan of it might well have prevented that subsequent failure of nerve; a failure of nerve from which he hadn't yet recovered even after five years?

Or had I often spent more than I felt I could get away with on their Christmas and birthday presents although frequently I had done pretty damn well in return? But then, naturally, I *was* the youngest wasn't I, I *was* the baby of the family? And even as an adult . . . when wedding presents also had to be included and then the snowballing presents of a rather surprisingly chuffed uncle . . . well actually in all fairness I suppose I might have been growing a little more generous even before I'd cast in my lot with you Brad but that didn't exactly turn me into a John D. Rockefeller.

So no. Plenty of practical jokes, in retrospect mostly unfunny and even unkind . . . yet, apart from being the resident family buffoon and sometimes, at table, drawing off my parents' anger from whoever might have been temporarily out of favour, I couldn't recall one single really *brotherly* thing which I had ever done.

"As good a brother as you could possibly get." She even has to repeat it.

And yet . . . And yet it could have been so easy. I wasn't ill-natured. I wasn't (particularly) slothful. So what then had stopped me? I wished to God I had been brotherly. At that minute it seemed the most important failure of my entire life.

But even yet Sarah hasn't finished. "I know I speak for both my sister and my brothers when I say how privileged we feel to have had you with us Danny. Even for such a relatively short time."

"Hear hear!" calls out Rachel.

"Hear hear!" cries Barnaby.

"And maybe it's true what that old cliché says." Simon; Lambretta-balked Simon. "Though I've never understood why it should be—and have to add still don't. But here's another very strong piece of evidence to support it. So perhaps . . ." His voice breaks in the same way that Sarah's had. "Perhaps the good do die young."

Oh Christ.

What's more, people on every side are murmuring their assent.

I seriously think have I descended into hell. Almost seriously think it. He goes on to make a big deal out of some bit of really ancient history when he and I had been playing in the woods and come across a smeary trail of blood which we'd decided we had no option but to follow. It led us not to a human body but to that of a pitifully trembling and rolling-eyed fox who'd plainly been run down whilst crossing Bounds Road then painfully dragged itself over this instinct-driven short distance in order to die. Tearfully we'd hunted for some sufficiently stout stick. But in the end Simon couldn't bring himself to use it; we'd been terrified we were either going to botch the first blow—or blows?—or hear the skull crack and see the brains spill out. Afterwards in spite of none of these fears being *quite* realized we'd both been very sick together, really pretty violently sick, Simon just as much as me—"a real example of fraternal bonding," he now terms it, "fairly basic I'd say." This raises a slightly shaky laugh somewhat comparable to our own on that long-ago day when we'd thought we might be tracking murderers and stumbling towards a possibly headless and otherwise dismembered corpse. All the emotion being generated—expressly to mock and punish me it seems—again makes me wonder if the devil himself doesn't have a hand in it.

"And my darling I'd like to second everything that Sarah and Simon have just said."

My mother—well of course my mother; Satan would scarcely have neglected the opportunities afforded by a grieving mother. Not only is her son aware he doesn't deserve such eulogies; what's worse he also knows it really wouldn't have taken that much effort to begin at least partly to deserve them. *I wouldn't have needed to be a saint to have still come a lot closer to this astonishing guy everyone's inventing.* And it isn't as though I'm stupid. Maybe not wonderfully educated but certainly possessing an average share of native wit. And added to that—at any rate theoretically—a Christian. Why hadn't I *seen*? Just answer me that please. Why on earth had I not seen?

She goes on.

"We do indeed feel privileged to have had you with us my darling. And yes the good really do seem to be taken from us young. What more can I say? Your life was an example. And anyone who knew you, even briefly, realized you were special. We all loved you—very very much." Satan has obviously advised her that if she wants to produce the fullest emotional impact she should follow Sarah's lead and speak to me directly; and oh sure you have to admire the guy—how does he work it that she isn't instead producing the deepest and most cringe-making embarrassment? People appear to be sincerely moved, don't keep their eyes fixed firmly on the floor nor look as though they're likely to congratulate themselves afterwards: "My God only suppose that we'd begun to giggle . . . !" And all of this for *me*. "I can tell you darling there won't be a single day of my life when I don't remember you with all the love I feel for you right now."

Oh bullshit Mum. I love you too, dearly, but just listen to yourself. Please. This is me, this is Danny. Why are you talking in this way? My life was an example all right—no question. But of *what* may one ask? Of unremitting blinkeredness? Of waywardness and wasted opportunities?

And just hang on a moment! Hang on! What about Brad? Since Sarah nobody has mentioned Brad. Fuck it his parents supplied all that champagne which you all have in your hands—and a lot more with which to give you refills. Yet anyone who didn't know would suppose that I was the luminary around here and Brad was just my acolyte.

Because it's me who's still being celebrated: currently it's Sebastian and Sally and Laura from the hotel who are all having their little word. (And bless them they're sweet; in other circumstances I'm sure it would have been fun and gratifying to hear them and I know that later I'll appreciate their good intentions and their obvious affection. *But*—once again *but*.) These three are followed by Martin Frobisher from school—we've met perhaps a dozen times over the past eight years—what does *he* know about the way I lived my life? Then there are the kind Miss Cottons who've supplied the tea. You'd think that I'd popped in to see them regularly to mend fuses, replace washers, unblock drains; to read aloud *A Christmas Carol* while they sat with their embroidery before the fire. In fact I had done each of those things *once* (the book admittedly spread over several evenings); this was the only way in which I could ever have been thought to eclipse you, my love, no matter how faintly—somehow I had always had a gift for getting on with old people, particularly old ladies, which despite the origins of *A Hundred Years Hence* you didn't altogether share. Then there's the vicar Mr Kenworthy putting in his own few words—Mr Kenilworth who so far as I can remember never even met you. But where are all the people on *your* side—yes I know I'm making this thing sound too much like a wedding—where are all your longtime London friends? Where are our host and hostess from the party on the night on which you died and at least six or seven of our fellow guests? Where are all those people you felt close to in the theatre and where are all the down-and-outs from across the length and breadth of the land who never once held out their hand to you in vain—and who at one time might even have had business cards left in their palms as well as money? And where is Hélène? And where Suzanne?

And on the other hand—in my case the utter reverse of all of this—where's Philip? Where Jonathan (whose principle defect was merely his lack of age)? Where Mr Tibbotson? (Dead of course: at a bit of a disadvantage.) And where all those countless down-and-outs who never once held out their hand to *me* and found themselves rewarded for their pain? (Well 'never once' is maybe overstating it but only very slightly; 'hardly ever' would be fractionally more correct.) Why don't such as they, those countless down-and-outs at least, now cut a swathe through our sitting-room lugubriously reminding each damp-eyed mourner that inasmuch as I hadn't shown any compassion towards *them* what earthly right did I have to hope for, let alone expect, any to be shown towards *me*? 'I was a stranger and you took me in . . .'; the quote goes something along those lines. My Macduff-and-Banquo-type accusers, many of whom have doubtless died from disease and exposure and lack of sustenance, would probably have learned the rest of it and could probably now declaim it with conviction and majesty and resonance.

Hell it seems like some conspiracy. This is *your* house we are standing in; indirectly *your* champagne that is being drunk. By rights it should have been your commemoration a great deal more than mine.

I've had enough of it. I go upstairs.

In our bedroom I lie on the bed—my side of it. Then I move across to yours, wanting to see things as far as possible exactly as you yourself would have seen them: the underside of the light fitment with its metal clusters of overhanging grapes plus trailing leafstalk (sounds kitsch but isn't—you the grandmaster of non-kitsch); the small threadbare patch in one half of the claret-coloured Victorian curtains, a flaw we'd been meaning for a long time to have invisibly mended and which is noticeable at the moment even though the curtains aren't drawn; the smile of the fat cherub at the top of the gilt-framed mirror (okay, a *fraction* kitsch) whose gaze was levelled marginally more at you than at me. I jump up abruptly and pull back the counterpane, let my own head rest on the pillow where yours last rested. Turn and press my face against it. You very often slept that way—I thought I remembered you doing it for some of the time last Friday night—lying on your stomach with your hands clutching either side of the scrunched-up pillow and your nose buried somewhere in the centre.

Oh Brad.

Brad.

I'm sorry for that farce downstairs. So well-meaning but so . . . so laughably selective; and though in some sense genuine . . . so laughably false at the same time. I wish the picture that it gave of me was true. I wish that you, not I, had been the focus of it. And above all else—I so much wish that you'd been here to hear it with me.

Time passes. I get up and wander round. Just touching things. Your things. Go inside the study. Sit in the armchair near the window where in the evenings I sometimes sat reading whilst you—obsessed—worked fluidly at the computer. Normally when I wasn't on duty we'd spend much of the evening on the couch downstairs watching a DVD or some programme on the box, frequently I with my head in your lap, frequently you with yours in mine; but from time to time the characters in the play you were writing simply demanded to be listened to and have you transcribe their words even after seven o'clock—and well after seven o'clock—when more typically at that hour we would decide the sun was over the yardarm.

In any case always before we went to bed you'd read to me the work you'd done that day and over our ritual nightcap would often amend things according to my suggestion.

"Yet don't ever think you're going to wrangle your name onto the playbills as co-author; I'm always fiendishly possessive of my babies. On the other hand though—when at last it comes to getting the script published . . ."

"Some fulsomely heartfelt dedication?"

"Possible. Just possible. How fulsomely heartfelt would you want it to be?"

"'For Danny. Always fiendishly possessive of my babies.'"

I may have been a little drunk; that wasn't at all the kind of thing I usually said. Highly unliberated. Even you Brad looked a bit surprised. (Though on the whole quite pleased.) In any event by last weekend the play still wasn't finished: the twist ending—dramatic, poignant but mildly funny too—not fully worked out to author-satisfying standards. Despite your death, however, the chances are the play will be produced. The chances are it will get published. The certainty is . . . there'll be no dedication. But I now feel wonderfully glad I made that tacky tacky comment.

And do you recall this further snatch of conversation?

You had said:

"Always my very greatest fear—well, within reason—is that I should die whilst still at work on something. I don't demand to be there for the first night though I think I might regard it as a bit shabby if in fact I wasn't; but I do pray that every word and almost every comma will be satisfactorily in place before I have to wing it. And preferably I won't have any other plot in mind that's starting to excite me."

"Well thank you very much!" I'd declared. "You don't think anything of leaving *me*! Just some bloody uncompleted play."

And I'd brought you down onto the floor in the sitting-room and sat on you and tickled you and made you retract—or at least add to—the expression of your very greatest fear.

"Remember," you'd cried out between your yelps and pleas for mercy, "remember . . . I am . . . nineteen years older than you! And while you treat me like this . . . am no doubt aging rapidly. But. When finally I do have to leave . . . I promise you . . ."

"What?"

"I'll expend more thought on you than ever I did on any of my plays. Will that do? Does that atone?"

"So so. Not bad—for a pagan!"

"And one day . . . at your own appointed time . . ."

"What?"

"I'll come back for you."

"Oh, now, that's just a little too glib! Judge me an innocent? You're only pretending to believe."

"Not so, not so." There were tears running down your cheeks. "You know when I'm being tickled I could convert to practically anything."

And eventually we'd stood up. "All right," I had conceded, "I'll take your word for it. But please don't let me down."

I'd added: "Of course it rather assumes we're still talking to one another at either of our appointed times."

"Which I agree is a pretty rash assumption; especially if you continue, my lad, in such sadistic ways." I remember you'd been brushing yourself down. "But I do implore you Danny—the next time you feel impelled to act like that—first to think about whether there might be any play in progress."

"And whether or not, I suppose, you might have another plot in mind that's starting to excite you?"

You'd put your arms about me. "I have to admit it. Whatever your more barbarous inclinations you're at least a fast learner."

And whether or not you might have got round yet to making out your will. No. Thank heaven. I had so very nearly said it but now couldn't feel sufficiently grateful that at that final teetering turning-over second something had stepped in to prevent me. Something—God, good sense, my grandmother? It hardly mattered what. Money was the one thing which you never wholly learned to laugh about. Though I truly do believe that in time I might have got you there.

Not money precisely. My own questionable attitude towards money. It was the one point on which you didn't fully trust me.

(But you could have done; you could have done. It was always you I cared about, you idiot, *you* not your silly money. I somehow feel it in my gut that even if you'd been poor, really poor, dependent on state benefits or something, I just feel it in my gut that we would *still* have got together, got most euphorically together, to share the sort of love for which I would have followed you to the ends of the earth—if ever strictly necessary—even though I knew when I got there I'd only find you in your catalogue clothing, even though I knew when I got there I should still have to face the world in mine. And I don't mean just catalogue stuff either, charity shop would have done. But yes all right I know: as I must have told you a million times before, so easy for me simply to say something, my eyes all wet with sentiment, when there's now no earthly way that I can give you proof. I don't suppose you'd ask for proof any longer; or maybe ever would have. But I only wish there could have been some. For my own sake rather more than yours.)

And money was the very thing of course which precipitated our two deaths. The love of money being the root of all evil. But it was *my* love of it—if anyone's—and how unfair of God to punish *you* for that. Particularly at a time when you hadn't yet finished your play.

Yes Mum my life was a very fine example.

All right, all right. Once again I know. Free will he'll say. God will say. Say it all comfortably. Sitting back with his feet up. Sorry boys but you're well aware there's got to be free will. And try to be honest about this. You wouldn't choose to be automata any more than I'd choose to have you so. Surely?

Right then God. So far so good. But if I ran the world I'd devise some plan whereby the decent people didn't have to suffer because of the free will of the bastards. Haven't you ever thought of that?

Oh but I suppose blasphemy can hardly constitute any proper answer. I'm sorry God.

I'm sorry Brad.

But in any case Brad please don't go so fast that I shall never catch up with you; or at least not catch up with you for a long time. Oh please. Can't you see how very much I need you?

It's all a bit ironic really. You told me you'd come back for me but in fact it doesn't work like that does it? Shame! I would give anything I had—which I know of course is nothing—to see you walk into this room. Then we could go on together hand-in-hand and I should never again, ever, ask for any other single thing. (Though I seem to have made that promise once before. Maybe more than once.)

From downstairs now—perhaps from someone standing on that very spot where we once wrestled—I suddenly hear laughter: either some heavenly comment on that potentially hollow pledge I've just made or a sign that the meeting below me is beginning to chill out. I return to the sitting room in time to see your Scottish uncle, with the help of Mr Kenworthy, folding up copies of the national broadsheets: *The Times* and *Telegraph*, *Guardian* and *Independent*. And on over-hearing a scrap of someone's conversation I quickly realize what's been happening. Your uncle has been reading out from your obituaries. Probably everyone in the room has already seen at least one of these for himself (stupidly somehow I haven't given any thought to your obituaries) but I get the impression that all four of them have just been read in full and each one, in this very sharing context, pondered and appreciated. (Damn it, then, why couldn't I have come down a bit earlier!) Apparently the piece in *The Times* actually suggested you might have been in line for a knighthood—or anyhow thoroughly deserving of one! I don't think my family ever recognized just how highly you were thought of in some quarters. I used to proselytize like mad but naturally you just had to thin down all my rhapsodies with your boring old modesty although didn't I keep *on* telling you that people would only take you at your word? Besides which of course a prophet in his own country . . . or even in his partner's country . . . !

But at least I've come down in time to hear my father say, "Yes like Tom joked just a minute ago I wish I could have seen these obituaries long before Brad had to die. Hearing them now I feel immensely humble. For although I valued him highly I clearly didn't value him enough. I wish I could have had a second chance."

It's an unrehearsed little speech and some might understandably find fault: the idea that a person's worth can be increased only after you've learned the views of the professionals. But I'm not prepared to feel that sensitive about this; I know what Dad was trying to say.

And it's directly afterwards that the toast he proposed earlier is finally taken up. The climax to the whole occasion. Soon everyone will start to take his leave.

"Raise your glasses please and I repeat it. *Bon voyage* to the pair of them! The very best journey any of us could ever possibly imagine!"

Well it's hardly likely to be that is it? But I go and kiss my father on the cheek and thank him. Do the same to my mother and to the rest of the family; and to everybody else as well. Thank them both on my own behalf and yours—though I hope this doesn't sound rather too much like the Queen being gracious. "Have a happy life; see you in heaven": a sort of general wish.

"My goodness." It's one of the three Miss Cottons—Miss Hester Cotton. "Is it only me being silly or does anyone else here feel it?"

Those nearest look around inquiringly.

"Danny seems at moments just so close," she says. "Danny *and* Brad. Both of them. So *very* close."

17

I WAS ALONE IN THE HOUSE—with the tables cleared, the plates, cups and glasses all washed, the downstairs carpets vacuumed; everything put back to rights. Mainly by my own family. Sadly though when they had left they had taken those four newspapers—or at least somebody had. That was disappointing. So what was I to do now? Return to Richard and Isabella; report back for my next set of instructions? Yet neither of them had intimated that I should and I simply didn't feel like going back. No. But for the moment I didn't feel much like going forward either. It was more than a sense of apathy which had over-taken me. It was darkness and depression.

Earlier I had professed I was in hell when having to listen to all those things that had been said about me. *In hell*—what an imbecilic sort of expression; so impoverished, so totally bankrupt; it was like when people spoke about the cross they had to bear: how arrogant, how smugly unimaginative . . . how impossibly cheapening was *that*? It was only my self-disgust that had been talking though; my growing awareness of just how much I loved my parents and my siblings and of how much I was going to miss them, the realization that while I'd had the chance I had never properly appreciated them. All that and my disappointment over not finding you here. I might have claimed in my juvenile self-dramatizing way that it *felt* like hell but I knew far better now.

For this stealthily augmenting and solidifying depression made me almost wonder if I was ever going to find you again? Anywhere. Perhaps it wasn't meant that I should catch up with you? What had I known about hell an hour or two ago?

What did I know about it now?

I decided to switch on the TV. I stood in front of it and merely channel-hopped.

(And who knew, I thought sardonically, perhaps that was the way some message would finally get transmitted? *Proceed to the Shop at Sly Corner or the House on 92nd Street. There you will be met by . . .*

My luck was surely in! (Still sardonic you understand.) There was a western showing on TCM.

I would lie on the sofa and make believe my head was resting in your lap.

I looked for the remote; that was one of the things we were always looking for—with each usually blaming the other for its absence. However, secretly we both knew it was your fault you basically untidy git. (You basically untidy git whom not so very secretly I loved. And do love. And shall love. For ever and ever amen.)

I found the thing, increased the volume and returned my attention to the screen. A ghost town—I thought at first it was a ghost town—with tumbleweed rolling down its main street and precious little sign of any townsfolk. I wondered if maybe there was going to be a shootout.

But a shootout usually came at the end of a movie and because the camera was still pulling back in a very leisurely style it seemed more like a beginning—yes hadn't I even caught a word or two of exposition? Obviously it couldn't have been *Autumn 2005* but very much that kind of thing: a place and/or a date, first in blazing red script, then running down the screen like blood.

Before long however the camera came to a standstill.

Outside some run-down sort of rooming house.

18

I SUDDENLY KNEW WHY I WAS THERE.

Beyond question.

Proceed to the Shop at Sly Corner or the House on 92nd Street. There you will be met by . . .

But somehow I knew this wasn't just a place in a movie any more.

And equally I knew it wasn't anywhere that I would find my friend Clem sitting back with his feet up in the sheriff's office. I knew that it was literally miles away from any place like that. Miles and miles away. Maybe on the other side of the universe.

This was the Rooming House from Hell.

Or more exactly—make the definite article indefinite and change the preposition to 'in'. (And yes now I'd got it absolutely right. This was the real thing. No overstatement. No self-pity. Nothing.)

I had to go inside; I had no option. The lobby clerk was reading a glossy-paged magazine when, with my shoulder, I'd pushed open the swollen front door and approached the counter behind which he sat. I suppose they might have had sex magazines in the Old West too but the glimpse I caught of this one, even in the present murky light, seemed entirely modern. Certainly this pasty-faced unwholesome-looking specimen of roughly my own age was so immersed he scarcely even bothered to glance up.

"Yes? And what do *you* want?"

"I'm here to see Mr Tibbotson."

"Why?"

I found I was in no mood to be conciliatory. "Quite frankly is that your business?"

And now he did look at me. Our moment of eye contact made me feel quite sick. "All of it's my business. Every bloody fucking detail."

"Your brother's keeper are you?"

We stared at one another; my revulsion only fuelling my hostility.

"Yes as it happens. Yes!"

Then he shrugged. Shrugged his exceedingly narrow shoulders.

"Oh anyway who gives a shit? Smartass. You're welcome to that toe rag. You with your posh la-di-da accent. Room 5 second floor."

Perhaps he thought he'd been a little too forthcoming. He spat as if to conceal an overgenerous nature. The spittle missed my trainer by an inch. I hoped The White Hart in Uckfield—especially when I myself was on the desk—had seemed just a fraction more welcoming.

Second floor. Room 5. I knew that the man who came shuffling to the door had died while he was still in his thirties. Less than ten years ago. Now, like someone else I had only a vague recollection of having come across quite recently, he could well have been getting on for seventy.

He was gaunt, pale, haggard. Stooped. His sparse blond hair, several shades lighter than my own despite its matted greasy dirt, had at sometime been pulled back in a ponytail but had largely worked loose of its rubber band and now fell in lank strands. His clothes were filthy and they stank. Or he did. Or the room did. Most probably all three.

My first words caught in my throat while I tried to adjust to this further air of fetidness; the rest of the house had been a long way from sweet-smelling.

"Mr Tibbotson. You won't remember me. I'm—"

"Daniel Casement," he interjected in the flat reedy voice which more than his appearance, more than the brown tweed jacket and the light grey trousers, the white shirt and maroon tie, put me right back into that classroom in Nottingham where I'd most often heard it. He spoke the name with no suggestion of pleasure, nor even with any discernible surprise—although I suspected it had never been within his nature to show much surprise at anything.

And I could hardly have expected pleasure, could I, whatever the gaps in his present social calendar?

Indeed perhaps only because he'd been conditioned not to leave a visitor standing on the doorstep did he grudgingly invite me in. It was a courtesy I might willingly have dispensed with; the staircase and the landings, as I've said, seemed marginally less foul.

The room had mouse droppings scattered across its bare boards—along with other kinds of detritus. I saw this even by the dim wattage of the naked light bulb. There were no curtains at the window but the encrusted dirt on the glass threw everything into premature darkness—I guessed it was probably mid-afternoon—even though there'd been no hint of sunshine in the street. A half-filled bucket which you'd think most people would have covered, or at least tucked away into a corner, appeared to contain more than just one day's release of urine.

Of excrement as well. Some of it—or all of it—had floated to the top.

We sat on a pair of creaky chairs beneath the flyspecked bulb. Thank God he offered no refreshment.

"So *you've* been sent here too?" he commented at last—and in those few words there was, undoubtedly, pleasure. "The great Mr Daniel Casement, the boy we always deemed most likely to succeed . . . since he was unfailingly so good at pushing past, or knocking aside, anyone who stood in his path."

This onslaught took me unawares. And his tone wasn't flat any longer. Similarly at school the only times it hadn't been flat were when shot through with either vitriol or pain.

"Who's we?" I asked.

"Everybody. Certainly all of us in the staffroom."

"And is that really how they spoke of me?" He nodded with clear satisfaction. "But I thought the teachers—I thought most of the teachers—"

"Liked you? Yes. I'm sure that's what you thought. You always had that overweening ego."

I truly didn't recognize this as being a valid description of myself; either at school or in the years that followed.

"You've no idea how sickening it was to see you flash around your sex appeal—or what you must have thought of in that way. It was all a bit pathetic really. One can see that now."

I said nothing. It was true I could remember consciously employing charm on occasion, to achieve whatever I was after.

"Yet somehow you acquired this little gang of simpletons and sycophants. A gang whose every member was unpleasant though not nearly up to your own level. God how I hated having to teach the form which most of you were in! Always I had to pause outside the classroom before I could finally bring myself to open the door and stride in looking confident."

He had never looked confident.

"But you got at me," I said, "from the very moment you walked in. Just couldn't seem to leave me alone. Seemed positively to want me . . . I don't know . . . *want* me to be unpleasant."

"No. No one asks to have his life made miserable."

"Well anyway. Whatever the rights and wrongs you clearly got the whole thing so tragically out of proportion. I was only a—"

"No one asks to be driven to the point of breakdown. No one asks to be hounded on towards despair and suicide."

Oh come off it I wanted to say. You can't offload that kind of crap onto me; one silly little schoolboy can't be held responsible for a grown man deciding to put his head inside a gas oven. (And hadn't he even taken off his jacket and tie before he'd done it I wondered.)

"And even now it doesn't end. I am *still* in a state of despair. Thanks to you. What's more—it never will end. Here there's just no let-up. No way you can destroy yourself and finally have done with it."

And it was all there in his expression: he wanted me to know precisely what I'd set in motion, wanted me to know that it was merely a beginning, there could be no idea of my ever—*ever*—being able to atone. I must remember him for all time.

"So what price happiness?" he asked. "What price eternal peace of mind?" Yes he was talking about *me* now not himself. And he actually laughed as he did so, laughed quite wildly. He showed his greyish tombstone teeth; he showed the craziness in his gunge-filled eyes. I swiftly looked away.

But it was scarcely more comfortable to glance about the room. You saw at once what he was up against, or some small part of it, you saw at once—

"Don't even think it!" he exclaimed. "Don't even think you can *begin* to understand!"

I nodded guiltily.

"To mention," he went on, "only a couple of things. Which still won't give you any understanding—but it could maybe bring me a measure of relief merely to talk of them. Even to the likes of you."

He scratched his head reflectively. His fingernails were jagged—dirt-rimmed—and I again averted my eyes, pushed back my chair a little, to avoid all those airborne flakes of dead skin I could imagine whirling about me.

"Every day and almost all day long the man in the next room coughs and hawks and clears his sinuses. You think that isn't much? The walls are paper-thin and you just sit here and *wait* for that following small explosion. Then every day around this time he somehow stops it for an hour or two so every day around this time my hopes get raised, I start to think Well maybe that's the end of it . . . I know of course it's not."

"And the other thing?" I asked, after a suitable pause—which did in fact contain a good amount of sympathy. (How couldn't it have?) Not enough though. The sources of other people's irritation can never be as wearing as the sources of your own.

"The other thing: the two men overhead who were once tap dancers and who still rehearse their routines every night—*all* night—for all the world as though they're now preparing for a comeback. These are such petty things you're going to say. I can assure you they're not. Does hell accomplish nothing more you're going to say. I can assure you it does. Yet scarcely needs to."

"Then can't you speak to them, these men?"

"That wouldn't change a thing."

"Why not?"

"Just trust me—it wouldn't."

He then added however: "But still I think of them sleeping solidly throughout the day and so I bang upon my ceiling as fiercely as I can. Every half-hour or so. Yet neither this nor my neighbour's constant hacking—in which case I might have seen some point even in *that* . . ."

"Maybe it will stop sometime"—an immensely lame offering—"for some reason which you can't foresee. Maybe you'll get new neighbours."

"No."

"Why? How can you sound so sure?"

"You still don't get it do you? You don't even come within a mile of getting it. And I suppose you used to kid yourself that you were bright? Even the stupidest do that."

I gave a shrug.

"Because, you numbskull, the days in hell repeat themselves and repeat themselves and repeat themselves. Endlessly. In every dreary detail."

"But how can they? How can the days merely repeat themselves? The very fact we're talking to each other now . . . ?"

"You come here every afternoon."

"What?"

"And we always hold this selfsame conversation. Next I shall say to you, 'You've only just arrived in hell, you haven't got the least conception of the way it works,' and you will say, 'Then if I've only just arrived . . . ?' And I shall say, 'They always knew that you'd be coming. But they couldn't wait to reunite me with my greatest earthly torment, they gave me daily previews of how it would forever be.'"

I shook my head, in point-blank denial.

"Of course," he continued, "how do I know whether you're still merely a projection or indeed the bona fide article? I don't. But I suppose, when you think about it, it doesn't really make a lot of difference."

I did think about it. But it was extraordinarily difficult to get to grips with, and despite everything else I'd heard, my mind seized selfishly upon one isolated phrase.

"But how can *I* ever have been anybody's greatest earthly torment? I simply don't see it."

"That's what you always say and I assure you that you may not have meant it and would probably never actually have wished it on anybody, not even such as you would wantonly have done that, but all the same . . . And then you say, 'I don't believe in predestination, just can't, just won't!', and I say, 'This isn't a matter of predestination, it's only a matter of foreknowledge,' and then your poor butterfly mind, always unable to settle for too long on any single point of discussion, flits away from that one and you say—"

"But this time I'm real. This time I'm real! This time I'm here!"

"Exactly."

And he again grinned his death's-head grin—with what again could have been taken for genuine enjoyment.

"Yes. And how are the mighty fallen! Eh? I'll wager that you— *you*—never supposed your life would end in failure."

"No—and it didn't either." Sympathy was one thing; but I was only prepared to extend it so far.

"Indeed, end in the greatest failure of them all," he said. "Just like my own life did. Just like mine! In the end you came down to the same level; you can't much like the thought of that! *Us* with a common bond!"

Yes surely his pleasure now was genuine. Even in hell you could experience pleasure maybe so long as it sprang from a sour source.

"Oh the great Daniel Casement! Opportunist, sexpot, golden boy! To finish up his days a weakling and a loser—a fucking all-round big-time loser—weak through and through for all the world to see! A *suicide* no less!"

"No!" I shook my head; shook it vehemently. "That isn't how it was! That isn't at all how it was!"

How openly he was gloating! Plainly he felt no interest in trying to disguise it. "Oh yes my friend. That's always how it is. Terminal illness or annihilating failure. People will readily admit to the former of course but seldom to the latter. Look at you: a case in point. The fact that I admit to failure makes me—in that alone if not in countless other ways—wholly your superior, poor self-deluding clown."

I said: "Mr Tibbotson I'm afraid you've got it wrong." I thought I had rarely heard such coldness emanating from my own voice. "Shall I tell you why I killed myself? If you must know I did it purely out of love. Otherwise what? I'd have needed to go on without the one person who meant more to me than life itself. Frankly no contest; I couldn't have faced it."

"Oh out of love?" he said. "How sweet! How very touching! How syrupy and spineless! Or in other words—how pathological! How neurotically and morbidly dependent! 'No contest' you say? *That's* what you couldn't face: the contest that everybody's life becomes when they find they have no one but themselves to rely upon." His jeering rose another octave. "But to try to make out you died for some great transcending passion—pure cinema! Romantic tosh! Aimed at the stupidest most sentimental audience. Not worthy I'd have thought even of you."

A cockroach plopped into my lap. The small shock I experienced was well-timed: at least it gave me a chance to cool down and tell myself if it consoled him to believe I'd ended my life in humiliation and defeat—well what did it matter, let him enjoy whatever scrap of comfort he could find. I merely said, as I very cautiously resettled after shaking off the cockroach: "Is there no way then of breaking out?" I meant from the cyclic repetition we'd just been talking about—talking about for ten years now?—but he misunderstood.

"No. There's only one way you can ever leave this place." His tone seemed to grow even more disdainful.

I didn't know whether he was speaking of hell or simply of the rooming house. Perhaps the two were interchangeable?

"And what is that?"

"I'm tired of telling you," he complained—then stopped. Stopped in an attitude of some surprise. (So, patently, I could be wrong: sometimes he might have been known to show surprise.)

"I don't normally say that. Normally I . . . normally I just tell you."

I too felt somewhat disconcerted though for a different reason. His manner had unexpectedly softened; become almost friendly.

"Well?"

"But there was no one who cared for me enough." At first he said

this quite matter-of-factly yet then he repeated it—repeated it slowly.
I immediately knew why. He was paraphrasing his usual answer.
"Oh my mother of course. Everybody has a mother. And maybe the
younger of my sisters. And there was a girlfriend once but she went on
to marry someone else."

I didn't understand what he was saying. Yet I could see he was still
concerned with his experiment. After a moment I mentioned some
small discrepancies which earlier, naturally, hadn't occurred to me as
such.

"You told me that right from the start there'd been no deviations.
But a couple of the phrases you've used don't seem to bear that out.
'You come here every afternoon and we always hold this selfsame con-
versation.' 'That's what you always say.' Well obviously expressions like
these can't have been there from the word go. Can they?"

"No that's true," he said. Again speaking slowly. "Sharp of you Case-
ment. What's more—we've never spoken of such anomalies till now."

"So . . ."

Yet then his optimism faded; and that was somehow more pathetic
than anything I'd so far witnessed in this place.

"Oh but it's a trick," he said, "it has to be a trick. And when they
think they've raised my hopes sufficiently—it's like I told you earlier—
then they'll return me to my normal groove. In a second or so Case-
ment you will start to scratch. I shall speak the one word: 'Fleas.' 'Oh
God!' you'll say and then we'll both be back on track."

We waited for a minute in a state of shared suspense: me wholly
determined not to scratch—him equally determined, I felt sure, not to
supply any explanation. But as we waited I began to want very much
to scratch; and in several different areas too. Yet feasibly this could
have been nothing but the power of autosuggestion. (Or maybe *not* so
feasibly: in view of the room and its insect-ridden verminous condi-
tion.) At any rate I asked at last: "Why is that relevant? Anyone who
cared for you enough?"

Then before he could answer: "Is that a question which I normally
put?"

He shook his head.

"Enough to do what?"

"Take my place."

"You mean when they die?"

"*Naturally* I mean when they die!"

The return of his contempt reinvigorated my own. "And you would actually let them do it? Your mother? Your sister? Or in fact *anyone*? You would actually let them take your place?"

"Oh yes oh yes oh yes! I'd almost forgotten: the unfailingly superior Daniel Casement; still so very much holier-than-thou at every turn! May I *respectfully* suggest something: that until you find yourself totally in somebody else's position you will strive always to do your poor limited best—hard though I realize this is going to be—simply to refrain from expressing an opinion? May I suggest that?"

"But even your mother or your sister!" I repeated, as though I hadn't heard a single word of that. Well it stood to reason: I wasn't a saint: if he must go on provoking me he surely couldn't expect me not to retaliate. It was the age-old pattern reasserting itself.

Yet I experienced some sort of mild remorse. It was partly true what he had said: you did have to walk that mile in another man's shoes. (In fact wasn't this one of the several platitudes which I had shared with Clem?) "You mean it's just as easy as you say? One dead soul can get another out, set another free? Then why haven't people drawn up some kind of rota system? Why does anybody have to spend more than an hour or two in hell? I'm afraid I really don't understand the logic."

Yes everyone following the example of Christ, I thought, and taking on the sins of his brothers—*And he descended into hell*—be it of course ever so briefly and ever so superficially. But at least they'd get the merest taste of it. Even if they could wave quite cheerily at Old Nick as they were doing so: "Just passing through you know . . . just passing through!"

"*I'm afraid I really don't understand the logic* . . . That's the way you used to speak in school."

Withering, withering! The bitterness seemed once again to have grown fixed.

"Which only goes to show," I said, "I'm still the same regular guy I always was."

"The same arrogant bastard who can't believe there's anything—anything whatsoever—on which he can't become an overnight authority. His first day in town and he expects to be an expert!"

"Hell's teeth," I shouted. "All I did was come here to apologize! After all this time don't you ruddy well know that?"

But now at least he did appear to be accepting that I was no longer just a ghost or a projection; that I was indeed the genuine article. I wondered if this meant the false one would automatically return tomorrow or whether there'd simply be a vacuum that would require to be filled some other way.

"All I wanted was to offer you my apology," I said again, more levelly. "The thing is—I've had you on my mind." Since when? This afternoon? Yesterday afternoon? I hoped I wouldn't need to be specific.

"That's nice," he said.

Sarcasm had always been his strongest suit.

Though after I'd heard that he was dead . . . I'd had him on my mind then too. For weeks undoubtedly; maybe months. I'd despised him but at least I'd thought about him. Felt sorry for things; wished I could have played them differently. Had felt that rather odd mixture of contrition and contempt.

But then bit by bit, of course, I had forgotten.

Had probably done my utmost to forget.

He asked now: "And what am I to do with your apology? Tell me Casement. What would you *like* me to do with it?"

"Accept it I suppose. Then try to forgive me for the way I behaved."

"Ah yes. I see. So suddenly everything will be all tickety-boo?"

I didn't know what else to say. I was very much on my own here. *Again* Richard or somebody—couldn't you possibly have primed me just a little?

"*Apologize?*" he said. Quite equably. As if meaning only to analyse the etymology. "But I must confess there's one thing about that concept which never ceases to mystify me."

I waited.

"Well in this case. How could anyone have the gall to imagine any apology appropriate? Let alone adequate? How could he believe himself *able* to apologize? In any way meaningfully? Sufficiently? Candidly, this problem perplexes me."

He lost that air of purely academic curiosity.

"Oh yes. Knowing you of old of course. How *could* I be perplexed?"

So once again I had to struggle to preserve my cool.

"At any rate I've done what I came here to do," I said. "And I'll repeat it if you like. I'm really sorry for the cruel and thoughtless way I treated you."

Also I'm really sorry for the way you magnified it out of all proportion. You were crazy and unbalanced, must already have been deeply disturbed to let it get to you as you did.

But I suppose I know absolutely nothing about the things that made you what you are. And if I really understood the nature of those influences and the nature of the personality they molded . . . *well isn't understanding tantamount to forgiving? (And you can't possibly be a lesser soul than whoever it was who said that—wasn't it a Frenchman?)*

"Also," I remarked, "I'm sorry that I appear to have taken up your time so needlessly throughout these years. Your 'greatest earthly torment'; that must have been difficult to cope with." Oddly I wasn't being ironic: I found quite suddenly that I had insights into just how difficult this must have been. "But do I need to stay here any longer? You could be snoozing, whilst the hawker remains quiet."

There was a further marked pause.

"No perhaps you don't," he said—and again the sheer novelty of it seemed for the moment to have brushed aside recrimination. "All this is new. We must put it to the test!" His voice became a whisper. "*Now!*" he said. "*Immediately!* Stand up and go!"

The whisper suggested I should accomplish this so stealthily my exit might—just possibly—escape everyone's notice. Even if only for a while.

But, paradoxically, now that I *might* be able to escape—just possibly—might be able to escape both him and his surroundings and fill my lungs again with comparatively fresh air, I felt reluctant to appear in too much of a hurry. Despite his own sudden urgency. Or even actually to *be* in too much of a hurry. My recent insights seemed to have enfeebled me.

"Except before I do go, how about your briefly helping me to try to understand the logic? Even on my first day. After all. You were once supposed to be a teacher weren't you?" This was meant to be said lightly but contrary to my best intentions (and I was now willing to believe that—yet again, *just* possibly—he too might have some mildly good intentions) it didn't come out in the slightest as it should have done. It was no good. He wasn't at all like Isabella. We were never going to take to one another.

He gave a lengthy sigh. "I haven't mentioned this but if you've killed yourself only somebody who's done the same can ever set you free."

Oh sweet Lord! And you'd even wish *that* upon your mother and your sister!

"Because suicides," he went on, "are the only people—apart from the irretrievably evil—who can be shown the pathway into hell. Indeed *must* be shown the pathway into hell. Also, like I said earlier, it needs to be someone who loves you, loves you with the sort of love I think that you and I have never experienced or maybe even heard of . . . outside of the cinema . . . because . . ." Yet it seemed to me he couldn't say the words.

"Because in order to release you the other person must agree to stay behind?" Well yes he'd already intimated as much.

I reckoned that my own idea of a rota system would have been better. But I knew the type of response I'd get if I repeated it. I said merely, "I would have thought that, anyhow, anyone who came here had to stay behind."

I had no notion what made me come out with that, except for the fact of my being distracted by endeavours not to answer his comments upon love. But having said it, and somehow having belatedly heard it, I instantly felt faint. I had to grab the edges of my chair—and even at that moment realized there was something nasty hanging from its underside. Felt faint . . . because until this very point the thought hadn't occurred to me: that once you were here that was it. No way out. You had to stay.

But his response brought with it greater reassurance than anyone could have imagined. Possibly hard to believe: I could almost have hugged him. Yet now only 'almost'; it wasn't like with Clem. However, my faintness was forgotten and my gratitude immense.

For he hadn't been obliged, even, to give *any* response. Not so far as I knew. He could have let me suffer.

"No. Don't ask me why. There are those of us who are condemned to stay. There are those of us who turn up merely on a visit. "

He smiled unpleasantly.

"I'm afraid, you see, that I don't understand its logic either."

"And you're saying I'm just a visitor?" Desperately I needed confirmation. (Already!) "But how would you know that?"

"Because otherwise you'd have been met, provided with quarters, kept under surveillance. Prince Charming on the door wouldn't have allowed you to come up here unescorted."

He paused to subject his no doubt flaky scalp to a second vigorous scratch. You'd not have been surprised to see those fingernails draw blood. "In any case I think by this time you are usually gone. *Invariably* gone. That oaf next door will soon be starting up again."

"Maybe he won't."

"Thank you for that abiding piece of comfort."

"I mean—who knows what might not happen now?"

"Yes that's clearly anybody's guess and very wonderful to think about."

"Are you in fact . . . are you sentenced to remain in this place for all time?"

"Yes."

"No slightest chance of a reprieve? As you've said—you're not an expert. Mr Tibbotson I could start agitating for a complete review of your case. I could couldn't I? I know people who might help us—people in high office—" I was actually thinking only of Richard—well, apart from my grandmother that is—although naturally I wasn't at all sure on what level of the hierarchy Richard functioned. But at least he'd be able to advise me and point me in the direction of the people I should really be talking to.

And then of course there would be Brad.

Excitedly, unthinkingly, I laid my hand upon the teacher's bony knee—and then realizing what I'd done needed forcibly to stop myself recoiling from the contact.

"*What* people in high office?"

"I don't know. We're going to get you out of here Mr Tibbotson!"

"Oh please go away," he said—now suddenly sounding not just weary but exhausted. "I can almost begin to think you may mean well."

"I do. I swear I do." *And always have*, I thought, but couldn't say it, since obviously there had been times when—stupidly, selfishly, unseeingly—I hadn't.

"And since this is possibly the last time we'll be seeing each other I'm inclined to say that I forgive you for what's passed—why not?—indeed, I think I no longer possess enough energy *not* to."

His tone was grudging but I still felt touched.

"Thank you sir! Oh thank you sir!"

I tried to shake his hand. But this remained limp and unresponsive.

"And since, too, that's the only thing you truly wished to hear, you may now go on your way rejoicing. You leave me marginally better off—no matter if it doesn't last, this break in the monotony. Such a thought should also make you slide down the banisters and sing out gaily as you go. Might even bolster your self-confidence a little which was always where your problem lay. You see—I even make a joke. So just go in the happy knowledge that I made a joke and allow me, as you said, to maybe take a snooze."

I didn't again attempt to shake his hand and he didn't even stand while I mumbled my goodbye but as I glanced back from the doorway he was already shambling towards the thin-mattressed single bed whose stained sheet and almost transparent blanket, inadequately pulled over, must have provided as much of a welcoming home to bugs as it ever did to man. For an instant I saw him sitting on the platform on Speech Day, in his gown and mortarboard, as erect and bright-eyed and well-groomed as any of those who sat on either side and I saw the incline of his head and tight-lipped smile as the colleague next to him made some small jibe or comment. "We're going to get you out," I repeated softly. "Before you know it I'll be coming back to tell you how." Then uncertain of whether I felt more saddened or noble I hurried down the stairs and past the spotty desk clerk who looked up from his magazine and must have been giving me his usual obscene smirk as I wrenched open the warped front door. In the deserted street and against one side of the building I had a long-awaited pee (you should've seen the state of the lavatory which on my way up I hadn't been able to bring myself to use) and thought again about the problems which beset me.

But they didn't seem quite so all-encompassing as before.

19

BEFORE YOU KNOW IT I'LL BE COMING BACK. Goddammit could I truly have said that? I was the guy who'd once remarked to Brad, "If people don't mean things they have no right to say them. This is a warning. Don't ever tell me you'll phone me this evening or tomorrow or whenever without doing it."

"You're *so* intolerant."

"Unless you've got some bloody good excuse," I'd added.

Some twelve months later Brad had appended a footnote. "We're the two most trustworthy sincere and utterly reliable people whom I've ever had the good fortune to run into. Forgive me if that's in any way tautologous. Who can be deserving of tautology if not such splendid upright folk as we?"

We're going to get you out of here. Before you know it I'll be coming back to tell you how.

We? Who's we? And how were we going to do it? And how long was 'before you know it'? And dear God please provide me with some answers.

Any, that is, apart from the glaringly obvious one.

I'd rather have 'Hypocrite' branded on my forehead. 'Be warned, you can never take his word for anything.' I mean literally—quite literally. Branded. Written with a red-hot nail. Without the use of anaesthetic.

Thereby agony undergone for an hour. Searing pain; discomfort—for a week? Shame and humiliation throughout the full remainder of your everlasting life.

As opposed to the daily replay of details that were dreary loveless and uninteresting even to begin with. For all of eternity, endlessly rotational, unstoppably repetitive—Brad forgive me if that's in any way tautologous?

Well strictly no comparison. Clearly. Torture is the easy option.

Even though I'm scared to death of pain.

Though why in the name of fuck am I even going on like this? Am I just trying to convince myself I've got a heart like anybody else and don't merely dismiss a matter out of hand . . . before at length I let myself dismiss this matter out of hand? Please Brad. Tell me what you think. Tell me it's the greatest load of crap you've ever heard. Anything. Just talk to me. I really do need to have you talk to me.

It really isn't any of my business is it? Still less any of my responsibility? How can it be? It may sound hard but in the last analysis Tibbotson's tragedy is simply that. *Tibbotson's* tragedy.

You always said that for an honest bloke I went in for such an awful lot of bullshit. You were right.

You always said it would have been nice if I'd finished my education; had really got to know John Donne and Alexander Pope and other minds as fine as theirs; had read some of the great philosophers and maybe managed in the process to discard a few of my more woolly ways of thinking.

You always said that one day I should honestly try to get off my backside and just do something about it.

And to think I actually put up with all that kind of talk! You wouldn't have found many as forbearing and as sweet-natured as I. As me? I love you Brad; love you, respect you, need you, want you. All the time; for ever and ever. I'd like to make you proud. I really would like to make you proud. Just tell me what I ought to do.

Well first and foremost get something to eat. I can practically hear you saying it. How you used to carry on—and *on*—about blood sugar levels, most frequently mine!

I looked about me. (Instant obedience!) Found a snack bar on the corner which wouldn't have won any prizes for hygiene nor have got written up in the Good Food Guide but the nourishment was free and—yes you're right—now if at any time I was going to need to keep my strength up. And if my mouth and teeth should afterwards feel furred with grease . . . well at least cholesterol isn't an issue I have to worry over any more, so there are blessings to be counted even in such a crude, ketchup-splashed—blood-splashed?—none too warmly recommended little eatery as this. (Well certainly not recommended by myself: you should have seen the way the plate was almost thrown down on the table, the cutlery picked up off the floor, the fork tines literally encrusted.)

Then after that the coach station.

The coach station is on the outskirts of town right at the end of Main Street. Here we're not talking Wells Fargo, more National Express or Greyhound. But who ever uses them? Are they there only to tantalize: so near and yet so very nearly impossible? Otherwise—well, what? Allegedly there are buses leaving for every destination known to man but the location of the countless bays is hopelessly confusing even when they're all as empty as they are at present. However by dint of much perseverance (and anyway having nothing else to do) I finally discover the embarkation point for Pack Hill tucked away between those for Manila and Santa Barbara. On the concourse there is often litter blowing round your ankles. Yet despite such frequent currents of well-nigh freezing air, jets of it almost, the atmosphere remains invariably heavy with the reek of petrol and vomit, a reek which sits on your stomach, stirs up its contents—in my case hamburger and chips and onion, half-cooked and probably done in lard—and is clearly self-perpetuating: it can't be long before even the most determined will add at least one further small puddle. Large puddle? I say 'invariably'. Following my meal at the snack bar I have spent more than twelve hours in this terminus and more than twelve hours spent in such a place seems practically the same as always. Supposing, I thought, this was to form a part of your cyclical hell: the time passed mainly on broken insanitary benches in a dark stench-laden terminal, with a stomach chill and a thumping headache but not so much as a moment's real sleep throughout the whole long night. The whole long night following on from the equally interminable late-afternoon and evening? It didn't bear thinking about. It just didn't bear thinking about.

It had to be thought about.

I told myself almost whimsically that it had to be thought about. Why? Because there wasn't so far as I could remember a single really worthwhile thing—both generous *and* disinterested—that I had ever done in the entire course of my life. Not totally, totally disinterested.

Would this one be disinterested? (I asked myself whimsically.) Even that guy in *A Tale of Two Cities* who knew he was doing a far far better thing knew also that he was heading for a far far better place. Not for him straight from the guillotine into a bus station. Or a room with mouse droppings and bedbugs and a pail of piss. (And worse.) *His* act wasn't disinterested. I'm not saying it wasn't very nice of him and all that but the thought of almost guaranteed gold stars must at least have momentarily occurred to him. In those circumstances, having myself led a thoroughly useless and dissolute existence, perhaps I too would have taken another chap's place in the tumbrels—especially someone's whose earthly life appeared so chock-full of promise. (It struck me that Dickens had somewhat stacked the cards but all right.)

Yet the difference was that *I*—here in another kind of hell, in fact the hellish prototype of every once-and-future variation—*I* would not be notching up any cluster of gold stars. There just wouldn't be a real incentive any longer. No praise, no rewards. If I chose to stay then that was it. I stayed.

And stayed for somebody whom I had never liked and whose own earthly life had never seemed to promise very much, certainly not from the outside. So why should his *heavenly* life merit outside sacrifice, anyone's, even mine? The spared man in the book had had a lover waiting. I had a lover waiting. Did Tibbotson?

But then I remembered that the sacrificing fellow in the book hadn't much cared for that fellow *he* was liberating; and besides—as he would no doubt have reminded himself as he moved forward to redemption—judge not lest ye be judged and in the eyes of our maker every one of us is just as precious as absolutely any other. (Undiscriminating or what? Take even me and Brad.)

Not that the *lest ye be* would need to worry me any longer; any more indeed than high levels of cholesterol. I smiled wanly. That on its own should feel quite restful. (I whimsically informed myself.) I'd always worried a little about being judged: being judged in heaven just as much as—or maybe rather more than—being judged on earth. This certainly hadn't stopped me from behaving badly; consult Mr Tibbotson; but usually (and most typically until I went to sleep that night) I had at least worried about it.

Perhaps my greatest danger at the moment consisted in my trying to prove—but only to myself, I didn't care (well not too much) about Tibbotson—that I was a good bloke; had it in me to be a wholly unselfish human being. Almost Christlike; in this one and totally isolated instance. Special. For me there was something terribly seductive in the notion that in one good act, outstandingly good act, I could conceivably justify my whole existence.

So even now it wouldn't be disinterested. No way. Of course not. I simply mustn't lose sight of that important fact.

Important? Essential!

And while it was true that in one sense anyway my whole existence had already been justified by Brad I still wished I had gone to Rwanda at the time of the genocide or to Kosovo in all those months of civil war or to any place where there'd been almost unimaginably appalling conditions either man-made or natural and where any bright and able-bodied person could possibly have been of life-saving assistance. Thailand, Pakistan, the Niger. Of course (that sad refrain running throughout so much of my recent life) it was pathetically easy to say this now when I no longer had the chance—any more than I had had the courage or the altruism when it could perhaps have made a difference. At the best I had only been an armchair hero; paving the way for a terminus-bench wannabe. Both equally useless. But I wished it had been otherwise.

One can always wish it had been otherwise.

Presumably Brad would mourn for me if it was borne in on him at some point that I was now never going to catch up with him. But heaven—though naturally I wasn't at all an expert on this subject, let me be the first albeit regretfully to have to admit to that—heaven wouldn't in the least live up to expectation if unattached people who didn't positively choose to be unattached needed to remain so. (And could there in all honesty be many, or even any, who positively *did* choose that state, I mean long-term?) So there had to be upmarket introduction agencies or singles bars or dinner parties designed with that one same sweet objective: no messing around: partner matched perfectly with partner to ensure an absolutely wonderful first date—and each subsequent meeting only compounding and improving on the last. Oh God! I felt jealous already. In the light of what might just conceivably be about to happen would the mere two years which Brad and I had spent together in the temporal world come gradually to seem almost insignificant by all eternal standards? A rather quaint prelude, even fairly cute in its own small way, but in contrast understandably very thin, understandably extremely shallow?

No! That was it. That made up my mind for me. I'd been talking almost as though I was really going to go through with it but I saw now there was obviously no chance. Sorry mate. Just me and my usual trails of fantasy. Sorry about that. *Before you know it I'll be coming back* really meant nothing more or very little more than *See you, see you around sometime!*—just a thoroughly ordinary form of leavetaking. Final assessments of a person's true integrity didn't ride on whether that person actually saw anybody again after he'd unthinkingly said See you! Surely? It was in fact the kind of casual farewell which I myself had often made to people whom I scarcely knew.

"See you!" "Be seeing you!"

Yes mate—really truly sorry. Almost touched base. The only mercy is you'll never know how close you came.

Poor old devil.

But let's face it you poor old devil: a lot of it's your own fault anyway. It's not as though (I imagine) there aren't any facilities here for washing and shaving and trimming your nails. Supposedly you must have arrived in your present state but then you could have spent your first day giving yourself and your room and your self-respect a thoroughgoing repair job. That's what I'd have done. And I'd have whistled as I worked and I'd have sung and I'd have danced. (Those two guys upstairs clearly had the right idea; I bet they feel quite jolly as they go through all their tap routines; I hope they chose the right music to dance to.) I'd have had only humorous positive thoughts. Throughout the day I'd have told Brad repeatedly how much I loved him and appreciated him and how enormously grateful I'd always feel for the way in which he'd changed my life. I'd have read something that repaid constant re-reading. I'd have—

I suppose I'd also have had to clean up that blocked and excremental lavatory. God! Imagine having to spend a substantial part of all recurring time in trying to sanitize *that* without (most probably) any of the proper cleaning materials, not even a pair of rubber gloves. And think how mucky you were going to feel after you'd done it—assuming of course that you could do it; how deep-down mucky and contaminated. *Were* there any showers? Were there any showers that wouldn't need something of the same treatment and from which you could actually expect a decent flow of water rather than merely a rusty trickle—along with a decent adjustable temperature instead of one either permanently scalding or unthinkably icy? This after all was hell. In hell, I sorrowfully began to suspect, an all-singing, all-dancing, all-*zestful* lavatory attendant was going to be a bit difficult to come by . . . even with myself so merrily in line for such a topnotch inspirational job.

Oh hell. (*Not* a pun.) Why can't you just get a move-on you wayward bloody bus? For Pack Hill or for London (Golders Green, Marble Arch, Victoria) or for absolutely any bloody place on earth. Manila, Santa Barbara, Alice Springs—who cares?—I'll make my own way back. Just hurry up and *arrive*: first bus for any destination so long as it will only get me out of here.

I supposed he could answer, Tibbotson could answer, that he had been despairing. You don't dance and sing and whistle when you're in despair; you don't seek out the shampoo and conditioner or think about your cuticles. I supposed he could answer he didn't even know about this cycle thing; that he had thought he had more than enough time in which to get going with his mop and feather duster and in which to ponder colour schemes.

More than enough time. Eternity.

I supposed he could ask me what relatively few pages of the same book or books repaid *that* much re-reading: three thousand times over up till now. Well roughly that is. Give or take.

I supposed he could argue that the only insights you'd ever receive from the re-reading of those relatively few pages even after three thousand times (give or take) were the very same insights you'd have received on your initial reading. The only addition to your every thought on that first day would have been the knowledge that you were going to think it again.

And again.

And again.

I supposed he could ask me where I thought I was going to come across that book or those books in the first place; or where the guys upstairs were going to find their records or tapes or CDs.

And perhaps there was even another point he could have contested. I had ascribed a lot of it to being his own bloody fault but he might have replied that he'd never actually *asked* to feel ground down beneath the weight of his despair. "Oddly enough Casement that was never absolutely my aim. Even when I didn't realize everything that it would lead to." I really hated—how much I'd always hated—that combination of stingingly sarcastic tone and flat and reedy voice!

Oh shut up I said. Shut up! You were a whingeing old fart then and you're a whingeing old fart now. Why can't you just have the decency to shut the fuck up? *Please.*

20

I SAW HIM ALMOST DANCE, I actually saw him almost dance as he went hurtling off, nearly dancing off, in the direction from which I had so recently arrived. You wouldn't have thought there'd be sufficient strength in those thin bones and shuffling feet to hurtle or to dance. Almost dance.

He didn't once look back.

"Ungrateful sod isn't he?" announced the clerk. We stood together on the rooming-house doorstep—no stretch of the imagination could call it a hotel—and he had the warty little fingers of his right hand gripping the bicep of my left arm as though those warty little fingers would really in any way have been up to the business of restraining me if I'd suddenly decided to make a run for it.

He'd presumably brought me out onto the doorstep just because somehow he'd known that Tibbotson would not look back. Or could he only have guessed it? This was the very first time in a whole long line of freshly endless days—a precedent, a landmark—a day so far unique in the whole history book of hell.

"Well smartass. Whose keeper am I now?" I must say he looked well pleased with the exchange; but then of course he would have shown himself as undiscriminating as God if he hadn't. His warty little fingers were still gripping me in a way I knew had nothing to do with security. He was simply feeling my muscle.

I decided to make a run for it.

21

IT WAS HARDER TO SHAKE HIM OFF THAN I'D THOUGHT—he was a wiry little bastard—but my initial advantage of surprise plus a fist aimed with all my strength at his solar plexus did finally dislodge him and I left him sprawling in some pain on the sidewalk because my knee had also met up with his groin. Welcome to hell I wanted to say. (In my posh voice with its la-di-da accent.)

Yet I didn't waste time on the civilities. Concentrated solely on running. My night on a series of hard benches had left me feeling stiff but at least I'd had enough time and gentle exercise to loosen up again. Luckily too I'd avoided breakfast at the snack bar so I wasn't weighed down with insufficiently cooked meat and gristle which one hoped was purely animal but in any case was surely designed to bring on indigestion. I managed to run fast.

I ran in the opposite direction to the coach station—not because the coach station was the one place a fugitive would normally make for but because I didn't want my pursuers catching up with Mr Tibbotson and returning him into custody in lieu of myself. I made sure my would-be jailer noted what escape course I had set.

I saw him stagger up. I heard him blow a whistle. The whistle triggered some alarm system which wailed immediately throughout the town. The hitherto deserted main street soon grew populous. A posse had been summoned: prisoners whose stupid dehumanized faces betrayed an eagerness to use whatever makeshift weapons they could find—against a fellow inmate, against anyone. I walked amongst them, these men and women pent up far too long, and hoped my sweat and heavy breathing would be put down only to the excitement, practically sexual excitement, that now seemed prevalent. Today was in the nature of a holiday—a hugely unexpected public holiday. They should have fêted me, borne me aloft, carried me off to the border; not wished to prove themselves so worthy of a privilege that had briefly commuted them from convicts into bounty hunters.

Into bounty hunters given dogs. Before Tibbotson had been released a piece of my T-shirt had been cut away and placed on file; purely a formality—it hadn't been envisaged how quickly this formality would serve. But that piece of T-shirt held all the scent those dogs were going to need.

Whilst they were being rounded up, though, I had thankfully made progress. A stealthy form of progress. But I'd got to the termination of the main street; found it became a road that ran perfectly straight over endless miles of scrub and wasteland. I had veered to my right across the scrub.

Some of the bushes and the stunted trees might—just—have offered me protection from merely human eyes; yet by then I'd heard the baying of the hounds. By then too I was really straining but presumably this also applied to my pursuers—less used to liberty than me. Perhaps I could ease up slightly?

Yet I soon realized that I couldn't: I'd assumed the dogs were leashed and being held back; but why? Why on earth? More likely they'd been given their head and until their handlers caught up would either surround me and snarlingly hold me at bay or else launch themselves at my throat knowing instinctively they'd got *carte blanche*: no matter how they tore I shouldn't be allowed to die; they could inflict the ravages of death without at all providing its corollary—a merciful extinction.

Mercies did exist however; even here. There was a stream that I could wade along—which naturally slowed me down a lot though I could still half-run.

In places the stream was fairly deep, a foot or more, and fairly twisty, and when I eventually stepped out of it I felt confident my scent could scarcely have survived. Indeed I knew it hadn't: I could hear the yapping of those fallible frustrated hounds and imagined how they must be rushing round in circles some half a mile behind.

I'd left the stream on the same side as I'd entered it and hoped everyone would suppose that, because the cover grew more plentifully on the other side, I would of course have headed off in that direction. Quite obviously the hounds wouldn't pick up my tracks again over there but if in the meantime I were just to double back blending my new scent with my old I could then at some point simply take a running leap across the road: the kind of long jump I'd been so justly celebrated for ten years ago—remember, sir?—oh I'd had lots of hero worship on the sports track! And at least since then I'd kept in shape. Both in the gym and the back garden.

Anyhow that subterfuge still lay a little way ahead; or I mean with any luck it did. Right now my pursuers came pounding along the bank of the stream making straight towards me. The dogs jumped up amongst them eager for direction. Not wanting to run the risk of movement I was hidden behind the one proper tree the area had to offer. The tree was slender and weedy but it was still the obvious hiding place. (Without I hoped being *too* obvious, to people thinking I was on the other side.) They came within some fifteen, twenty yards. Then after pausing in a rowdy halt to stare about them and engage in brief excited consultation they headed off *across* the stream. Praise God.

I let a good five minutes elapse, waited until they were virtually out of sight. Then I ran back to the road and stayed on it for possibly a mile before I made my jump. It wasn't a bad jump: fuelled by urgency and naked fear. Now facing away again from where I'd started out that morning (can anyone imagine the relief?) I struck off this time to my left. The land was flat and largely barren but I thought I'd probably be all right until tomorrow; because early though it was the light appeared already to be waning: hell's one fringe benefit for fugitives. But tomorrow of course—surely having guessed by then what I had done and surely with the smell of me renewed in the nostrils of their hounds—my hunters would be back.

With that one unforgettable proviso.

If tomorrow ever came.

Or to put it another way: would I begin again in the bus station or was it only the first *full* day of an inmate—a name now entered in the files—that got to be repeated?

And could the dispensation for such a vast and exultant body of searchers be extended over a fresh tomorrow as well as a fresh today?

(I wondered if fifty or more futures would now need to be re-channelled; and almost by definition this meant improved. That would be good. Hey now. That *would* be good.)

But who knew—who knew?—and in my current state of uncertainty I thought I'd better reckon on having tomorrow and (if providence were kind) the next day too to see what distance I could put between us, me and that vast body of searchers, for otherwise what difference would it make, three miles away or ten? And even if I couldn't escape this whole damning and benighted jurisdiction there might still be certain compensations. At any rate eternal repetition of an open-air existence—one spent mainly on the move and hopefully unmonitored—had to be by far the better option.

Naturally I didn't know if I was travelling in the right direction or if indeed there even was a right direction. I vaguely hoped that just as there were many roads which led to heaven there might be many roads that led from hell; and in fact I saw it as an encouraging sign that, towards nightfall, the scrub began to change into greener and more fertile land. The fields were untilled but I came across abandoned farm buildings—in one of which I decided I'd take shelter—and even found an ancient fruit tree: ate three small apples that were tangy and sweet; would have picked a fourth but didn't want to risk diarrhoea. The night was dark but I had seen—during that enormously prolonged period of dusk—that the countryside beyond the fields showed signs of growing hillier. Which was great. All afternoon I'd felt so vulnerable on level ground: an easy prey to strong binoculars. Now suddenly the outlook seemed more promising.

And maybe partly due to this and partly due to all my exercise I quickly fell asleep. That wasn't all. I slept well.

Moreover. In the morning I awoke to—

Well hallelujah!

Yes. Hallelujah!

But in fact I'd slept almost too well; made a much later start than I'd intended. Didn't even stop to pick more apples.

Yet it soon occurred to me I couldn't distinguish any baying no matter how I listened. Then had the posse been called off? Was that possible? No second day of bounty hunting filled with its own villainous excitements? But this could only be if there was something that improved on it. I caught another sound and after staring into the sky for ten or fifteen seconds was able to identify the cause.

A first helicopter was followed shortly by a second. And yet more shortly by a third.

So? Attempting to hide inside those farm buildings would be useless—they'd be the first things searched—and throwing myself onto the earth around them would be equally inadvisable since a white T-shirt (no matter how grubby), blue jeans and blond hair would all show up against the dried-out soil and stony grass of what I'd taken to be fields. There were some scrawny bushes I could try to reach but of course they too would make a thoroughly expected hidy-hole, as well as a largely ineffectual one. My only hope was an outcrop of boulders I thought I could discern in the distance. Undoubtedly I should be seen long before I gained it but if I weaved sufficiently I might avoid making myself too easy a target for either bullets that would stun (else seemingly shoot dead, why not?) or for any sort of animal-entrapping net which could be lowered by a trio of machines working together. Perhaps I had developed an overactive imagination—okay, admitted—but when it's the forces of damnation which are chasing you it's maybe forgivable to grow a little paranoid. I'm not convinced that I was growing paranoid.

The boulders themselves clearly wouldn't give much cover but something about the lie of the land made me suspect that they could form the entrance to a canyon. I wasn't able to feel sure but there did seem to be a track which might be starting downwards at that point.

Helicopters couldn't enter a ravine; not if it was narrow enough. And on this side of it there mightn't any longer be a place sufficiently flat for any of them to land. I felt I was being looked after.

Then I wondered if the planes were carrying passengers and whether in that case the pilots might shortly lower rope ladders. *Oh stop it! Stop it!* You might be fighting for your life but in some ways it was surely better to underestimate not overestimate your enemy's abilities; otherwise your every endeavour could appear so futile you'd at length be tempted into wholesale surrender. "Just come and get me. Here I am!" There'd be such a huge relief in that.

But if it *was* a canyon—and the indications all looked increasingly good—first I had to reach it. Briefly looking up as I ran—and weaved—I saw that the pilot of each machine appeared to be alone and to have no ray gun or revolver. In fact the demeanour of all three seemed curiously unthreatening. Their faintly smiling salutes were obviously ironic but at the same time they weren't at any pains to head me off and one might have thought that—instead of trying to intercept me—they looked rather more intent on behaving like sheepdogs. So they were either stupid or friendly. Yet both options struck me as unlikely. I hoped there was a third: could they possibly have misjudged the width of the ravine? Maybe it was arrogant to question the judgment of professionals but there was no denying the fact that once inside the gorge they'd have remarkably little room for manoeuvre. If I suddenly decided to backtrack how easy would they find it to reverse? I might not achieve a lot by doubling back yet on the other hand... Or perhaps they'd anticipated some such strategy and only one helicopter would give chase; the other two would wait outside. It was all too complicated; too many intangibles. Besides. My only real alternative was to carry on.

To carry on towards the canyon. The sweat by now was coursing down my face, stinging my eyes and blinding me for many anguished seconds at a time; it dripped off my neck and arms and made my T-shirt heavy. My lungs felt close to rupture or collapse and as though they couldn't any longer survive the tearing strain of even one more shallow refill. Oh, come and get me then! For pity's sake. Let's have it over with.

But suddenly the shale or gravel was sliding underneath my feet. Suddenly? I'd so much thought I wasn't going to get there, it was like at the last I'd been moving only automatically.

What's more, they could certainly have followed me in. The gorge was steep-sided and narrow but I was sure there'd have been room. Yet now that I'd discovered my own miscalculation it also seemed as if they themselves had blundered. I was left to get my breath back and to negotiate the pass in freedom.

Or hadn't they miscalculated? Could they be playing some little game? Perhaps they knew very precisely what they were up to—had faithfully fulfilled their instructions. I didn't dare believe they could simply be watching me walk away.

But then again . . . Even the powers that be were clearly not infallible: hadn't they allowed me to make a break for it in the first place? And the fact that they had brought into play *three* helicopters, not merely one or even two, three helicopters in addition to the previous day's dogs and commandeered auxiliaries—mightn't this mean that I was getting pretty close to escape and they were growing seriously alarmed?

Also, even if they caught me they must be aware that constant daily exercise following a night of decent sleep represented far less of a penance than the one they'd have wanted. Wanted for *anybody*; least of all a rebel! Worse—because of course I'd know the outcome of the chase—even its original terror would have been removed. And wasn't exercise itself now seen as being the most effective means of dealing with depression?

Praise God. I felt very nearly in high spirits. In one way or another they had definitely slipped up.

Maybe I had simply to come out at the other end of the pass and that's where I'd regain my freedom; that's where I would find the pathway back to all the better things. Maybe I'd already won. That's why the pilots had been waving—a surviving touch of sportsmanship intermingling with their mockery? A canyon or a mountain pass formed a natural kind of division: a natural sort of entrance of course but also a natural sort of exit.

Oh, zip a dee doo dah! Watch out for me Brad. I think I may now have truly turned the corner!

Except that . . . an unpleasant idea occurred to me. Supposing they brought those hounds to the mouth of the ravine and simply let them go? Was that their plan? The dogs mightn't be able to scrabble up the sides, I thought—but then again neither might I.

So I pressed on now; with greatly renewed urgency.

22

IT TOOK ME HALF AN HOUR to reach the other end. During this time the visible tract of sky turned from overcast to blue.

And I suddenly became aware of something else. I hadn't even known I'd missed it up till then. Birdsong. Robins, thrushes, blackbirds. Even nature itself appeared to be coming back to life.

No dogs! I was on my way out! Clearly. I was on my way out.

But I heard other sounds as well. I couldn't place them at first; not at all. The distant clash of metal, the distant cries of men? These came from ahead not behind. They might be something to be wary of but they didn't emanate from my pursuers.

Yet by the time I came to the end of the pass it was evident I wasn't hearing any form of celebration. I emerged from the canyon cautiously and saw before me a vast plain. Hundreds of men were engaged in hand-to-hand combat. I threw up on the spot.

The main weapons they were using were battle axes. Those and mighty leaden spiked balls swinging at the end of short chains. And there were many men who'd either been separated from their shields or whose shields had become so buckled they were useless; less a defence than an encumbrance. Not only these shields had been thoroughly mangled. I saw arms in much the same condition. Human arms I mean. Arms and shoulders. Torsos. Faces. Heads.

That was apart from those that were severed. I saw a score of raggedly bleeding stumps. And even as I watched . . . there, with one godalmighty swing, a stout plaid-stockinged leg all but hacked off below the knee . . . was I the only one being sick? The roars now were accentuated—the screams—the howling. The very plain itself appeared to vibrate; the main thrust of the action, the body of the massacre, tilted first in one direction then another, continually shifting as some retreated some advanced—fled, pursued—trampling on, stumbling over, both the dead and the dying, sliding through the pools of blood, slipping on the trailing guts. I should have moved, I should have gone back in the canyon. I felt incapable of movement, incapable of rational thought. Even while I cowered I was caught up, I'm not aware of how it happened. Suddenly I found myself right there in the thick of it, no longer a spectator, now a participant, my nose filled with the hot sweet rotten odour, my ears filled with the terrifying blast, my eyes as far as possible kept shut, my foolish feeble arms pressing protectively across my head. (*Protectively?*) But eyes had to open—automatically. Arms had to be brought down—automatically. I was knocked, spattered, fallen against; tried each time to save myself, God knows why, till at length I must have learnt, stayed down, played dead, face pushed against the sunbaked earth, hands returning to protect my scalp, to shield it from the thud of boots mere inches from my ears, the thud of boots from time to time in jarring contact with my neck and back and legs. My decision though remained good; I knew instinctively I shouldn't get far if I tried to stagger off. And my knowledge wasn't confined just to that. I now knew more or less the period from which this scene derived—this fearsomely reanimating imprint? And more or less the setting too. (Culloden? Bannockburn? Names that had hardly touched me during history class.) Half these men were wearing kilts.

No. At least as regards dates I must have absorbed more than I knew. Culloden had happened over four centuries later than Bannockburn. By then there'd have been muskets and far more sophisticated ways of slaughter. When I came round again (it should have been a mercy I'd lost consciousness but I couldn't see that it had done me any good) I at once heard musket-fire; or at any rate gunfire. I wasn't on the ground any longer; I was spread across a barbed wire fence. And when the mists began to clear I saw no further evidence of kilts. I had moved on: a hundred and fifty years or more beyond Culloden. And I had been taken down from Scotland altogether and into northern France.

A comrade must have heard me moaning or seen me breathing or something. As gently as he could he raised me off the barbed wire and laid me on the damp earth. The wire had driven through my T-shirt and into my stomach and I don't know what sort of mess had been made by the machine gun which had hurled me against it in the first place (I must have been retreating; in fact I now recalled the bowel- and bladder-emptying fear persuading me to turn about); I only knew that it was hurting. Hurting. Hurting. But teach a person to be kind: in the very act of trying to minister, my rescuer himself received a hail of bullets in his forehead, cheek and throat. His blood sprayed warmly down my chin and pieces of his teeth ricocheted against my chest. He slumped across my wounded legs but the yell I gave was as much for him as it was for me. Few of the yells I gave throughout the next four hours—or was it six or was it eight?—while I watched helplessly a thousand people die and tried to pray that all of them would find salvation; few of those yells were purely for myself . . . does there arrive a time when a person becomes so numbed he can almost forget about himself—when he becomes so much a part of what is happening that his own identity starts to meld with everyone's around him? I lay there on the muddy ground, cold and wet and hurting under that relent-less rain of shrapnel and machine-gun fire, and during that indefinite number of hours I died about a thousand times; but never, sadly, once.

There are other times however when you can't think of anybody but yourself. Or I couldn't. Move forward another thirty years or so. Another war. But this isn't on the battlefield. Further sophistication has partially got rid of battlefields in Europe. Further sophistication means some refinement in its instruments of torture. Axes are out. Knives and pincers are in—and trays of slim and pointed gadgets you might expect to find more commonly inside some operating theatre.

For these are Gestapo headquarters. I am strapped into a chair. My T-shirt's gone, my socks and jeans. I might have been wearing underpants but my underpants were shat again and even Nazi torturers can be sensitive to smell. I have been bathed and cleaned up to some extent (head repeatedly held beneath the water in the process) to prepare satisfactorily for my moment in the limelight. My couple of hours in the limelight. My wounds from almost thirty years ago—or is it only almost thirty minutes ago?—have wholly disappeared.

You remember me reporting a conversation which I'd once had with Brad? Of all the things I've ever feared the one that probably heads the list is physical torture. I can't even talk about what happened during that couple of hours. Not every second was devoted simply to inflicting pain. There were long minutes sacrificed as well to pure anticipation. And to the discussion of what it was one might expect. And to the forehead-sponging between instalments and to the bringing round after a faint. And to the wiping away of sweat and blood and mucus. There were even some frequent forays into light-hearted banter: a little joke to raise your spirits in betweenwhiles. My vomit was tenderly removed off chest and stomach—where had the food come from that I was capable of vomit? You can imagine the ribbing and the jollity when it was tenderly removed from groin.

It might have helped to know there was some point. If I'd been privy to top-secret information and the futures of millions had depended on my staying silent . . . that at least would have been something. I could have thought with every fresh wave of pain from which I had resurfaced, Maybe another million lives just saved? It might have helped; I somewhat doubt it—does pain become less painful in a worthwhile cause? Though it might have meant my railing at God a little less. But he deserved it anyway: how could he just stand by, how could he ever have just stood by? So easy merely to shrug and murmur something about free will and then sit back and take another sip of your hot toddy. And turn your eyes away. Regretfully acknowledge the existence of pure evil in the world. That somehow let God off the hook did it, somehow left him free of blame? Made his life more comfortable? Whilst for certain others: Violette Szabo—Odette Churchill—Ken Bigley—myself, right at this moment . . .

Also it might have meant my railing at Brad a little less; and he did *not* deserve it. But I was completely out of my mind—hysterical—demented. Damn you! Damn you! Damn you! Why did you just go off and leave me like that? You must have known how anxious I was to catch up with you? And don't you realize that none of this would be happening now if only you *had* waited for me? And don't you realize that I would certainly have waited for you? Waited for you forever. But me, I simply wasn't worth the hanging around for was I? Though you always said you loved me—asshole. And I really thought you meant it—asshole.

Asshole!

Yet perhaps that did help a bit—my being angry. Having someone to shout at and to blame. No matter how unjustly.

You probably didn't even know I was dead.

How should you?

But at least in fairness to myself all this was whilst they were working on my toenails. I couldn't call *them* assholes; that just got me another blow, another series of blows to my already broken nose and swollen lips; which might almost have been an antidote you'd suppose—but wasn't, really wasn't, not at all. (And to think that I'd once used to worry about my looks!) On the other hand they did enjoy hearing me swear lustily at God. And at you. Even encouraged it, with each new flourish of the pincers.

That was the climax though: those nail extractions. Even they felt satisfied by then. Or else exhausted. Decided finally that I might have had enough.

Besides of course. They had already mentioned this many times over; possibly a dozen. They knew we'd all be meeting up again.

Tomorrow.

23

IT WAS BECAUSE I'D DONE MY BEST to get away and flout the authority of hell that they were making an example of me; and would go on doing so in perpetuity. I had thought excruciating boredom was the direst fate a person could envisage. How was it possible I could ever have been that shortsighted, that naïve? Now I would so willingly have settled for pure boredom.

And yet . . . when I'd have thought I would never manage to sleep peacefully again . . . that very same night I slept well.

Almost too well.

Made a later start than I'd intended.

Couldn't distinguish the baying of any hounds but very quickly heard the sound of helicopters.

Didn't even stop to pick an apple.

24

THE DEVIL MAY HAVE PUT ME THROUGH THAT ONCE but I can't believe that God would really let it happen twice. It isn't possible. It surely isn't possible? I know I've been a sinner—yes obviously I have and how—but I wasn't by any means a Hitler or a Stalin or a Saddam Hussein. I can't be meant to go through all of that again.

There has to be a way out—oh Jesus there simply has to be a way out. Even if I knew I'd been sentenced to only one week of it, just six more days, this would undoubtedly be enough to send me mad . . . if madness were ever an option. But we're not talking about mere weeks—or months—or years. Nor about decades nor centuries. We are talking about—forever! *Forever* . . . when I feel I can't get through even one more day. Oh God. There *has* to be a way out.

Prayer? But that's what hell's about or one of the things that hell's about. Knowing the uselessness of prayer. Knowing you live beyond the realm where prayers break through or can ever get listened to. In concentration camps they must have had this feeling. But even in concentration camps there may have been—on occasion must have been—the shadowy glimmer of hope; a faint yet stubbornly surviving belief in better things to come; a something that provided strength.

We have examples of people who somehow clung to faith. It's difficult to see how anybody could.

But in hell . . . ?

I don't deserve to be in hell. That fact alone has got to get me out. If there's no ultimate fairness in the world then after all man can't be made in God's own image.

Because if God who is supposedly all-powerful truly desires to be fair—then ultimately there must be fairness.

And if there isn't, then man cannot be made in God's own image. QED. The best of men—though far from being all-powerful—at least *endeavour* to be fair.

The fact that I can even think this shows there has to be some possibility for change. I hadn't thought it yesterday.

So why then don't I stop to gather apples? Do I *need* to flee from the helicopters? Having gone into the canyon do I *need* to exit at the other end? Once I get swept up between the Scots and Sassenachs—from then on I've no choice, that's obvious. But up until that point . . . ? Why don't I go for apples?

I consider it carefully—and this, as I say, is evidence of the possibility of change; even in hell can there be hope? But I am programmed to escape: escape the dogs if they're being used, escape the fliers if the fliers are. I am programmed to run—and run—and run.

Literally so? I wonder about this. Has there really been time and opportunity to programme me?

Or . . .

Or could it in fact be something else? Could it be merely that it makes good sense to try to escape the dogs? For if I don't what happens? They either savage me or else bring me to bay. Whichever, I'm back in the hands of my captors, from there to be passed on for punishment. If savaged of course I'm subject to yet further quantities of pain . . . which might well augment my daily menu but otherwise won't alter anything. Similarly it makes good sense to escape the fliers, since my failure to do so—there, too—will mean a swift return to jail.

Yet if I really have some element of choice . . . then couldn't I *force* myself to remain inside the canyon? Now that I know what lies ahead, it would be idiotic—lunacy—not to focus every last billionth atom on avoidance. That canyon might even serve as a bolt hole: one among whose rocks I could maybe eke out some Robinson-Crusoe-type existence for the rest of time—apart that is from the hours spent getting there and the hours spent sleeping in the barn? Need such an existence be altogether joyless? Couldn't I try to profit from my own unstated advice to Mr Tibbotson: sing, dance, attempt to think positively? Even humorously.

More—I could sunbathe, do physical jerks, find makeshift weights to keep me healthy. (For what?)

I could invent and improvise in ways at present unimaginable. But Robinson Crusoe himself would have wanted to take stock before deciding what might or mightn't be imaginable. And if I could indeed manage to stay, possibly my days in the canyon would be sufficiently varied to stave off at least some of that hellish dreaded boredom. (Oh Lord! Was boredom *already* something to be dreaded once more?)

However if by that sheer expenditure of will I *can* remain won't the helicopters then try to flush me out—the helicopters or the hounds? All right; I shall refuse to budge! Whatever the unpleasantness which may result from this there'll still have been the pushing back of boundaries. I can hardly believe it. There *is* hope.

Or am I getting wildly—that is, groundlessly—optimistic?

No.

I am simply stepping out in faith. That is what I am doing.

And for the second time, sweating profusely, intermittently blinded and feeling that my lungs have reached the bursting point, I tear into the canyon.

Eventually I pause again and double over whilst gradually the pumping slows and the breathing grows less laboured. From now on I shall simply walk.

And as I say I'll try to stop. I've even planned where I shall try to stop. There's a place where—against the right-hand wall of the ravine—two boulders, set roughly four or five feet apart, obtrude onto the track. Yesterday it crossed my mind they might conceivably form a narrow room: a tiny three-walled refuge. Ideally I'd have liked them more centrally positioned since they're only a very short distance from that terrifying exit point. But, ultimately, even such proximity could prove beneficial. The noise of war will serve as grim reminder if ever I feel tempted to bemoan the tedium of sanctuary. And anyway why should I need to remain in that particular spot once my independence is established? For one day at least I'll have the run of the terrain.

What confidence—though perhaps only due to the fact I'd slept so well! A further restless night and my buoyancy might all have been destroyed?

Naturally the sky seen from the canyon is once more blue. Even at this depth shafts of sunlight still fall across my path. Birdsong returns: each chirrup corresponding to its counterpart of yesterday? Drawing closer to those two boulders (and maybe growing paranoid again) I suddenly wonder about the possibility of some force field I shouldn't be able to cross; then in a panic start to pray, totally forgetting that God apparently has no dominion over the devil—and that anyhow there was a lengthy portion of the previous day when I'd been telling him explicitly how much I hated him. But old habit dies hard; especially in emergency. And despite all the horrors of the world, I now remember the God who cured my brother Simon's meningitis and assisted me to win the long-jump championship, the God whom I felt performed any number of small things throughout my boyhood and early adolescence to convince me that he really did exist; a helpmate and a friend who truly cared. Events like my meeting with Brad had consolidated a slightly wavering belief: five seconds later he'd have left the pub and I'd have lost him. (If I *had* lost him of course I shouldn't be in my present pitiful position. But that doesn't change my thankfulness—not basically, no way—despite what I might say, or rather yell, under extreme duress.)

As usual I try to incorporate into my prayer all feelings of gratitude; which unfailingly include both Brad and my family. And my friends.

But now I've reached the stones.

So this'll be it.

Of course you can.

Oh Brad I can't.

Bullshit. Take hold of yourself. Don't even think. Just do.

For a moment I listen to the sounds of slaughter. But I do think.

I think about the battlefields; I think about the torture chair. I turn into my refuge, whip round so as to be facing outwards, brace myself between the pair of stones—and wait.

A side step executed in a second. I may have taken them by surprise. No force field.

But I suspect that if they pull me out a force field can be set there in an instant. And it occurs to me that to pull me out they may resort to some kind of suction device: a mini-whirlwind for example. Or in default of suction a mountain lion—a cobra—a tarantula? Again, though, I feel I should hardly be envisaging such way-out possibilities; and for the time being simply continue to brace myself between those rocks . . . as if for all the world I were Samson and about to push down the pillars of the temple.

25

HOWEVER THERE WAS ONE WAY-OUT POSSIBILITY which I had *not* envisaged. They say the devil can quote scripture. What they don't mention is that he's also pretty expert at impersonation. I heard my name being called. I had been there less than three minutes and I heard my name being called. I had expected force of some kind. I had not expected sweetness. I hadn't thought I might be listening to the voice of Brad.

"Danny? Can you hear me? Don't be scared. It's me."

I said nothing. My heart did all sorts of stopping, beat-skipping, soaring, sinking things; it must have run the full gamut. But even so I said nothing.

The counterfeit called: "You see, I didn't want to give you too much of a shock." (What the devil was he talking about?) The tone was tentative even though it next attempted humour. "Bring on a heart attack or something."

Brad wouldn't have said 'shock'; he would have said 'surprise'.

So I decided I wasn't going to provide the satisfaction of an answer; any answer. Did they really think I could be fooled as easily as this? To some extent I might have got the better of them but they must still consider me a very poor kind of opponent.

Good! Well that could work to my advantage.

"Darling it's me it truly is. I know what you're thinking. Since you died I've known everything you've been thinking. Every single thing. I've been with you every step of the way. Literally."

This was diabolical; and I wasn't the type who could keep quiet indefinitely, no matter how wonderfully frustrating I thought it would prove for the enemy. "You're wasting your breath!" I shouted back coldly.

And think now. What sort of sense would it ever make for Brad to be in hell? He had neither taken his own life nor was he remotely evil.

"Those aren't the sole requirements." God this was insidious. The person or the thing out there had even caught the underlying chuckle so heart-piercingly familiar. "There's another one: running in pursuit of somebody you love—somebody you always did love, deeply, but whom all the same you've come to love inexpressibly more with every passing moment. I told you I'd come back for you. I know you haven't forgotten it so I'm almost forced to conclude that you didn't take me for a man of my word. Despite tautology."

I wasn't sure how long I could hold out. Once more I braced my arms between those reassuring boulders.

"I can't come in," he said. "This is your final test. You need to trust in God and simply to step out in faith. Which we both know is a phrase you yourself have lately had in mind—and a precept you've been straining to put into practice right from the beginning. So come on. Show you're ready now to lean back on him *entirely*. You've shown love; you've shown hope; you've shown charity. Only one thing remains and then you're through."

I smiled very slowly. He shouldn't have said that. The counterfeit shouldn't have said that. I mean certainly not those first few words . . . which had rendered all the rest of it fallacious. And just at that very moment when I might actually have been weakening! Thank you God oh thank you God.

This slip suggested that—very poor kind of opponent or not—I was at least a little more alert than he was.

For had he forgotten? Scarcely three minutes ago? *You see, I didn't want to give you too much of a shock.* His exact words.

And the inference to be drawn? The obvious, indeed the only possible inference? That *otherwise* he wouldn't merely have called out from a distance in order to give me warning; he'd have charged straight in and thrown his arms about me; impatiently dispensing with preliminaries.

Besides the counterfeit was very nearly pleading. (What did that remind me of?) The counterfeit was almost holding out a bribe. This surely shouldn't be the way that good things happened.

No. I was steadied by the cool smoothness of the stone against my palms. I couldn't go back to Scotland. I couldn't go back to France. I couldn't go back to the Gestapo. There were those no doubt who'd been through similar experiences and had managed to retain their faith—their belief in the ultimate victory of good. I envied them this strength and was totally amazed by it, made to feel indescribably humble and undeserving, but I was not and never could be of such calibre. There were certain places in this world where faith just wasn't viable. There were certain places in this world where God had never been.

The counterfeit said: "Danny you're wrong. You know the Creed better than I do. 'And he descended into hell and on the third day . . .'"

For some reason I felt the tears begin to well. "Then what did he do while he was there? Pop out for an ice-cream sundae? If so I hope it gave him indigestion."

"It may well have done—what he did while he was there. Chronic indigestion. He comforted the suffering. He stood beside the torture chair and entered in and instilled that incredible strength you've just been wondering at."

Plausible. Oh, glib.

"Well in that case why has he broken me?"

"And is that how you truly see yourself my love? But just look at you! Fighting every single bloody inch of the way!"

Oh Brad. I am broken. What shall I do? Wherever you are—you the real you the bona fide Brad Overton—just tell me what I ought to do.

I hadn't asked this out aloud.

But of course that didn't make much difference.

"Listen Danny. Please listen. This *is* the real bona fide me. And when I said that stuff about not wanting to bring on a heart attack I agree it was just plain stupid. But there are three points you've got to let me make. Firstly we don't stop expressing ourselves badly just because we're dead. Not all at once. Secondly I think that even good things—if they happen too abruptly—can sometimes come as something of a shock. But I was nervous and I know I paved the way quite clumsily."

"Nervous of *me*? The man you claim to have lived with for over the past two years? Oh yes. Naturally. I can fully understand that."

"Nervous you idiot that I might say the wrong thing. Make a total cock-up. (As in fact I have.) But surely you must *know*: one always does get nervous with somebody one loves. Before the future's all tied up that is—while things could still go either way."

"And the third point?" I inquired. Dry. Deadpan. Conceding nothing. "You did say there were *three* points?"

"And the third point: we're on the devil's ground, remember. He's frightened you're about to get away and he's contesting it like mad. There's nothing he'd like better than to see me make that total cock-up."

"Which you said was already made."

"I'm hoping it's retrievable. That so far it's only partial."

"Anyhow. He's frightened that *I'm* about to get away then is he? So what about yourself?"

I'd kind of thought this was in the nature of a trick question. But I wasn't too sure how. In any case it was supposed to be ironic.

"I'm sorry?"

"I mean—isn't he frightened you're going to get away as well?"

"But no that doesn't enter into it. So far as he's concerned I'm just visiting. A free agent."

"Although he knows you've come to take me back?" I realized then that I had indeed set a trap even without being fully aware of what it was. And now I could really hear the note of triumph in my voice—was ever any note of triumph more completely and pathetically specious? "I assume then they never told you a person can only be released from hell when somebody cares for him enough to take his place?"

"Oh Danny do you think I don't care for you enough to take your place?"

"And would you even know what it involves to take my place?"

"Yes I would. As I mentioned, I've been with you every step of the way. Every solitary step of the way. In fact my own testing has been wholly tied up with yours, from the very first moment of the crash and even before you took your life—because it was known of course you were about to do that. Not by me though. I was dumbfounded, staggered, literally can't express the gratitude I felt, even if at the same time I would have given anything not to have you do it. But that's why I had to leave the Halfway House before you yourself arrived. Again I would have given anything to be allowed to stay but . . ." There was a pause. "So yes. Oh God yes. To answer your question—I do know what it involves."

"To answer it in brief."

"Yes. Always admirably succinct."

It seemed the two of us were enjoying a small joke.

"So in that case how could you ever have thought that you would get away?"

He replied very gently: "*I* didn't commit suicide."

"Throwing God's most precious gift back in his face? The ultimate sin? Even less forgivable than murder?" Again, though, my tone had aimed at irony. The counterfeit made no response.

But was he that? Was he? Oh *Brad* . . . Wherever you are please don't give up on me. If I have ever needed to know you're there I need to know you're there right now.

"That isn't the point," I said. "You're here in hell; *apparently* you're here in hell. That's what matters. So I need to have an answer. If you release me what makes you think that *you* can get away as well?"

"Oh my love my love. You ask one heck of a lot of questions! But then of course you always did. People used to comment."

Which clearly meant he hadn't anything to say to that last and truly all-important one.

"Oh why don't you just go home?" I cried. "Go home! Back to wherever you've come from! I really can't be arsed to listen to any more of your stupid damned lies. And besides." I felt less angry now than plain dispirited. "Even if you *had* been the real Brad this ploy of yours could never have worked. Do you honestly believe I'd have let the real Brad take over from me here? I know the likes of you won't ever understand this but you'd still have been wasting your time. Perhaps a crumb of consolation?"

He started crying. The counterfeit started crying for God's sake. I could hear it distinctly.

"Yes, shame," I said. "It sure is a hard world out there! Is Daddy going to be most frightfully cross with you? You'll have to make him see it was an absolutely no-win situation—even *he* couldn't have done better. Either that or else you've just got to take your medicine like a proper man."

I had reckoned this was the last weapon in his arsenal. Perhaps it wasn't, quite. "I love you so much," he said. "I love you so very very much."

Yes crocodile tears and crocodile sentiments but the thing was—he sounded so unbelievably like Brad. "Stop it," I whispered, "stop it, please stop!" I took my hands away from the boulders and tried to block my ears. I started to hum as loudly as I could. After a few seconds I realized what I was humming. 'Diamonds are a girl's best friend.' (Brad had often told me that gentlemen prefer blonds.) I went on for at least another half-minute.

Then I finished humming and also unblocked my ears. "And do we still find you there Mr Telepathy?" Unexpectedly, almost unaccountably, I realized I'd have been disappointed if no answer had come back. Relieved—yes probably—yet weirdly disappointed too.

He said: "'The only thing you have to do is brush up on your telepathic skills.' That's a quote—from not so very long ago. Do you remember?"

That hadn't been in my mind. It hadn't been in my mind at all. I hadn't thought of it even once since that moment he'd first spoken it. (Well, maybe once but only that.) There was more than mere telepathy involved in all of this.

"Of course I do. It was the night on which you died. Correction; forgive me. It was the night on which Brad died."

"That's right. We each thought the other had arranged for John to come to pick us up."

177

"I will say this for you: you've definitely done your homework." I almost added—*with a devotion beyond the call of duty*. It was quite true people used to comment on the fact I asked a lot of questions; Brad used to say it was because I was a writer. But this of course was what made the present lies so scarily persuasive: the way they adhered so closely to the truth.

For so much of the time. For so very much of the time.

"By the way, I never knew you sometimes read a Mills & Boon. I'm sorry you felt you couldn't tell me. Did you really think I might have minded? (Though I agree I would probably have teased you quite a bit. But in that department you always gave back as good as you got—*at least* as good as you got. Just as in every other.) And also . . . while we're vaguely on the subject . . . thank you my love for leaving a message at the airport for Suzanne."

"I'm not impressed," I said. "I am not in any way impressed. And please don't call me your love." I don't know why it was only at this point I had latched onto that and even to me I sounded prissy; like Doris Day in one of those sex comedies with Rock Hudson. "But if you really want to impress me . . . ?"

"Yes? *Yes?*"

I'd spoken recklessly without any real idea of what I meant to say. But there was something nagging at me; something hovering, yet again, just beyond the confines of my consciousness. And I had to admit that I was curious. No—curious was most definitely not the right word, nothing like it. But what I meant was: well there couldn't be one chance in a hundred that this man was genuinely Brad and yet while there remained even the faintest possibility of my being in any way mistaken . . .

Therefore I was praying again. Naturally. Seeking for a foolproof way to distinguish between truth and falsity and knowing as I did so that this would somehow be tied in with that elusive bit of recall. The trick would be finally to pin down the memory while at the same time concealing it from all hellishly canny thought-readers—a clause that was incorporated, very much so, within my current prayer. (And right now I was having to tell myself, *faute de mieux*, that prayers possibly could get through, because there was absolutely nothing else for it.)

178

So I tried to fill my mind with images suggested by that tune I had so recently been humming: images of Jane Russell and Marilyn Monroe blithely heading towards Europe and of some of their fellow passengers on shipboard.

"All right," I said. "All right. You've plainly genned up on everything that happened on our last night. Tell me then of one way in which you were untypically illogical . . . thinking back also to our *first* night and making a clear link between the two."

"Oh have a heart!" said Brad—said the man who was professing to be Brad. "No, come on Danny! That's really a bit difficult isn't it?"

"You think so? Mmm." A kiss on the hand may be quite continental—but diamonds are a girl's best friend.

(That wasn't on the boat of course; that was after Dorothy and Lorelei had got to Paris.)

"Don't forget that I had drunk slightly more than I should have. A hold on logic doesn't always survive so well under such conditions."

"Too bad," I said.

"Can't you give one clue?"

"No."

"Our first night and our last night together—a connection—something illogical—I thank you for that 'untypically' but sadly it's no more deserved than that kindly notion you had about me simply romping ahead towards judgment; for which I also thank you my—for which I also thank you; very gratefully. But Danny you've just got to help me out on this."

"Why? I thought you knew it all." And naturally that latest insidious manoeuvre had scarcely gone unnoticed. This man had very clearly majored in the art of self-insinuation.

A kiss may be grand but it won't pay the rental—on your humble flat—or help you at—the automat.

Mind you in all fairness it *was* a bit difficult. Had our positions been reversed I had to admit I probably couldn't have done it.

"And don't forget," he reminded me, "that only this morning you were importuning in the name of fairness. The best of men, you said, do at least try to be fair. And you should know. If anybody should."

"Okay! Okay! I'll give you a clue. One clue." Was there going to be

179

no end to all this blatant wiliness? (*Feminine* wiles my mother always called them.)

But really I supposed, deep down, there was such a big part of me that so incredibly much wanted—

"We were looking at the moon reflected on the lake and you said something which I found a little hurtful."

"I know!" he exclaimed. "I called you Narcissus! Darling I didn't—"

"No. Something *else* I found a little hurtful."

Men grow cold as girls grow old and we all lose our charms in the end. But square-cut or pear-shape these rocks don't lose their shape . . .

Oh God if it is Brad please help him. But if it's an impostor then let him recognize he's beaten, make him just give up and compel him to get the hell out of here. Because I know I've said this before but I really can't hold out much longer.

"Cheesy," the man said. "*The Watchers on the Bank*. You didn't like it when I said that titles given to pictures could be cheesy."

"*Were* cheesy."

"And I don't even know why I said it. Can't think what I could have had in mind."

Diamonds are a girl's best friend. But help that's the end of the verse; how does the second one begin? There may come a time when a lass needs a lawyer.

Oh please God. Please.

Please.

Please.

But diamonds are a girl's best friend. There may come a time when some hard-boiled employer—

"Pictures with titles . . . ? And now I have to link this up with something I said on our first night? Something illogical?"

"Not *illogical* precisely. More, like, inconsistent."

"Some comment I made at the Quebec?"

Thinks you're awful nice. But get that ice. Or else no dice.

"Or if not there . . . That little French restaurant we went to. With everything a bit fussy and overwhelmingly pink. You had your back to the wall—and above your head—"

Yes? Above my head . . . ? Above my head—what? *What?*

"There was that Manet painting . . . *Le Déjeuner Sur L'Herbe.*" He was now speaking extremely slowly. "And when you asked about it I didn't raise one single objection did I? I apparently accepted it as absolutely unremarkable that pictures should have titles."

"It *is* absolutely unremarkable that pictures should have titles. And if you suddenly thought the practice cheesy when we stopped beside the lake I hope you'll remember to tell Leonardo da Vinci that, if you ever happen to meet him. Or Titian or Rembrandt or whoever."

Yet now I was just playing for time. I'd set him a puzzle and he'd solved it. And I'd prayed about it and this is what had happened. So then, I thought. So then. So then.

And oh sod it I was thinking. If it should still turn out to be a trick . . . well then too bad too bloody bad that's all.

If it still should turn out to be a trick . . . well then so help me I should simply have to let myself be tricked.

But Lord I believe. Help thou mine unbelief.

"Yet it makes no difference," I said. "Absolutely no difference. Even though I may now be ninety per cent convinced that you *are* Brad . . . I'm still not going to let you free me."

For it had suddenly come to me afresh. Hit me in the stomach. No not simply in the stomach. Well below the belt.

Because no way—no way—could I go out to him. Exactly as I'd told him earlier (yet now there was no longer the same element of mockery) this was a no-win situation; totally and inescapably so. Either it wasn't Brad out there and I was back in the hands of the enemy; or else it was Brad—a Brad who had demonstrated incontestably, through his pursuit and his persistence, that he was hellbent on releasing me—and then it was he himself who must fall into the hands of the enemy.

And in fact (ninety per cent be damned!) I now believed it truly was Brad. I felt literally an ache at the mere thought he was so close. So unattainable.

"Go away!" I said. "Go away! You're boring me—you with your cheap little tricks!" And then noisily and desperately I returned to the beginning of that selfsame song while, every bit as desperately but a lot less noisily, I strained towards the safety of my refuge. Went in as far as I could go. Stood there—almost slumped there—with my forehead pressed against the rock face and both my hands once more obscuring sound. Heard only my own pulse and the relentless unfolding of Lorelei's simple philosophy—no longer being expounded out loud but still retaining all her single-mindedness and instinct for survival. I really hoped that by its termination Brad would finally have gone away.

Jesus if I could do it for Mr Tibbotson I could certainly do it for Brad.

I suppose that relatively little time went by. Perhaps it was a bit like that afternoon in Leicester Square of roughly two years before. I felt a sudden touch on my shoulder and spun round and he was standing right behind me.

All we did for a moment was simply gaze at one another. He was still wearing his dinner jacket, and though he looked even better in it than I remembered, a dinner jacket in such circumstances appeared ludicrous.

Our embrace was short-lived. When we came out of it he stood wiping away all those tears of mine which hadn't yet had any chance to dry—wiping them away on his knuckles—and then just holding me at arm's length and silently scrutinizing me once more, as though we had been apart for weeks or months not merely days. It had certainly *felt* like weeks or months.

Then we were back in a bear hug. Yet even now I felt constrained not to let this miracle engulf me utterly. I told myself I mustn't forget that it was actually no more than a very merciful interlude; a blessed stay of execution. (Though if such an interlude could turn into a regular daily occurrence it would all but remain miraculous and I thought then that I'd be able to withstand almost anything. Anything within reason.) "But Brad it makes no difference. I'm still not going to let you free me."

"You don't have to," he said. "You're already free."

I drew away from him; instantly suspicious.

"Well it's like I said. Our tests were intertwined. And yes until three or four minutes ago—obviously I've got to tell you this—I really did believe I'd have to take your place. But now we're both free. We've passed. Me because of you, and you because of . . . Darling we've passed! D'you hear? We have both of us passed!"

Yet monumental bore that I was or killjoy or whatever—and despite what seemed like wholly genuine delight on his part—I still couldn't feel unreservedly convinced.

"But wasn't I supposed to come out to *you*? Not the other way about?"

"That doesn't matter. You were absolutely on the brink. It was clear what made you change your mind."

This wasn't all however. Far from it. I framed my words slowly. "Yet how did you happen to realize quite so suddenly" . . . I almost said *conveniently* . . . "that you wouldn't need to take my place?"

But he gave every appearance of being able to take this in his stride. "Danny," he smiled, "just come along with me."

Then he took my hand and began to lead me out of the canyon. Even before we'd reached the exit I could see the plain beyond it lay apparently deserted; we might have been the only two people just then in the whole of God's creation. Unremittingly jaunty he pulled me out into the open—virtually to that same spot where on the day before I'd first thrown up. No trace of any vomit. There were again blue skies and birdsong and somewhere a dog barked and I could also faintly hear the murmur of a breeze as it ruffled the grass which had now sprung up out of that cracked earth—with wildflowers dotted in it, and burgeoning trees, and a river running through—but essentially a vast enveloping hush seemed to have fallen all about us. And it was only sometime then that it occurred to me I hadn't in fact been noticing the noise of battle for . . . well I couldn't say for how long but at the very least not since Brad had first identified himself: *Can you hear me? Don't be scared.* I looked round astonished at the empty flowering landscape and as I did so we stopped and his arms again encircled my waist. "Are you still doubtful?" he asked.

"Yes! You haven't answered me! And even despite all of this . . . so long as I feel you're trying to fob me off—"

"You really think I'm trying to do that my love? I really don't *need* to fob you off—not any more. And never again. Truly."

He paused.

"Oh by the way is it now all right to call you my love?" He gazed at me in mock consternation.

I said: "Oh by the way is it now all right to give you a belt across the kisser?"

"In that case," he continued, amply reassured, "I can tell you I received a message for you. That message itself has disappeared by now but if you'll please stop looking quite so cynical you'll see the manner in which I came by it. A manner which ought to strike a chord in you," he added drily. "I feel you were always the sort of fellow who looked for signs and seemed to think at one point that even a bit of skywriting would scarcely come amiss. Right?"

"You know damned well it is but—?"

I had already looked up into the sky. There was nothing.

But he pointed out the place where in fact it might have been—I *could* now see a hint of fading vapour trail.

"You're kidding me!" He mutely shook his head. "Then sweetheart . . . oh for Pete's sake . . . what did it say?"

"I feel you may have to cut down on your swearing a bit in the future. Maybe give it up completely?"

"Is that what it said?"

"No but it easily could have done."

I remembered—and felt guilty. For a moment, quite intensely guilty.

"What *did* it say?"

"'Welcome Danny. Well done!'"

"Christ!" I said.

"Er . . . ?"

"No, sorry! I meant . . . well I suppose what I really meant was . . .'"

"Yes *wow* absolutely," agreed Brad. "Double and threefold wow. Wow unto infinity. Mind you is that the best that both of us can manage? Two educated blokes like us?"

Though we hardly felt in the least bit educated. We felt as if our real education and real opportunity for growth were only just beginning. Brad could scarcely answer a single question concerning what was going to lie ahead. "We'll be finding out together," he said. "Which I for one don't have a quarrel with. Oh incidentally," he added. "*A rather quaint prelude*, indeed, *even fairly cute in its own small way*! Listen to this you numbskull. Nobody—but nobody—could ever have taken your place. Not ever. Remember that."

"Oh come on then. So easy to say. Yet where's the proof?"

But in default of being able to offer any—or anything at all, other than instinct, he said, certainty, a two-year fund of memories and an awareness of how we worked together, now compounded for all time by everything we'd just been through—in default of being able to offer me any proof he simply put his arms back round me. It wasn't only this huge sense of awe we were experiencing, there was sheer joy in it as well, confidence, hope, anticipation, a feeling of travelling along a road that could potentially lead us to endless perfection, endless bliss. "Thinks you're awful nice," he added, after a long period of silence.

"Thank you. You too."

"No I mean that was the next line of your song. Second time around. We don't ever want to leave things unfinished any more do we?"

"Brad will you butt out please. I would like to have at least a *little* privacy."

"It's all right. You're safe. Can't do it any more."

"Then all I can say is—thank God."

"Yes," he said. "Thank God. Let's go."

www.ingramcontent.com/pod-product-compliance
Lightning Source LLC
Chambersburg PA
CBHW030335180626
46810CB00003B/1370